Return to Tomorrow

(The Time Bubble Book 11)

By Jason Ayres

Text copyright © 2021 Jason Ayres

All Rights Reserved

This is a work of fiction. Names, characters, businesses, places, events and incidents are either the products of the author's imagination or used in a fictitious manner. Any resemblance to actual persons, living or dead, or actual events is purely coincidental.

Cover art by:

Daniela Owergoor

http://dani-owergoor.deviantart.com/

Contents

Chapter One - Thomas 1

Chapter Two - Ben 21

Chapter Three - Thomas 45

Chapter Four - Ben 62

Chapter Five - Thomas 81

Chapter Six - Ben 94

Chapter Seven - Thomas 112

Chapter Eight - Charlotte 124

Chapter Nine - Ben 139

Chapter Ten - Thomas 154

Chapter Eleven - Thomas 171

Chapter Twelve - Sarah 192

Chapter Thirteen - Ben 206

Chapter Fourteen - Thomas 229

Chapter Fifteen - Sarah 252

Chapter Sixteen - Thomas 265

Chapter Seventeen - Sarah 277

Chapter Eighteen - Thomas 287

Chapter One - Thomas

The memory of the day I discovered I was different from everybody else is indelibly etched on my mind.

It was a sweltering June afternoon in the beautiful summer of 1976 when Terry French fell off the climbing frame in the playground at school. The ramshackle construction of rusting metal bars and rotting wooden planks would have been instantly condemned by modern health and safety standards, but things were laxer in those days.

There was no soft landing for Terry on the spongy rubber material that constitutes the surface of modern play areas. He felt the full brunt of good old-fashioned tarmac that had seen better days. The faded, painted lines applied years ago were barely visible through the crumbling surface. Dandelions and other weeds were establishing themselves in the cracks. It was only thanks to sheer good fortune that no-one had injured themselves on it before.

Moments before Terry fell, I had been badgering the sole playground supervisor on duty. Miss Morris was a young trainee teacher who had drawn the short straw of keeping an eye on the kids while her colleagues were busy smoking in the staff room.

"Miss, Terry's going to fall off and hurt himself, you've got to do something." I watched as my classmate climbed onto the top bar of the frame. He stood up straight and balanced precariously on the narrow strip of metal.

"Look at me!" exclaimed Terry. "I'm Evil Knievel!"

He had persuaded three other boys to lie flat across the flimsy planks that formed the top of the frame. Anyone who had been impressed by the stunts of Evil Knievel on television would have guessed what he was planning to do. However, the teacher seemed uninterested. Why did I know what was going to happen, but she didn't?

"He's fine, Thomas, now stop pestering and go and play," she replied.

I knew that he wasn't going to be fine because I had seen it all before. He was going to leap over the boys, pretending they were double-decker buses, and injure himself in the process.

Sure enough, a few seconds later it happened, exactly to script. Although he had managed to clear the other kids successfully, he lost his footing on the landing side. He let out a piercing cry as he plummeted off the far side of the rickety death-trap onto the unforgiving ground, several feet below.

"Oh my God," exclaimed Miss Morris, finally waking up to the situation. Her language would have incurred the disapproval of the headmaster if he had been within earshot. Old Mr Millington was forever banging on about not taking the Lord's name in vain during morning assembly.

She ran over to where Terry had fallen. He was screaming in pain and it was easy to see why. His leg was twisted at a horrible angle. A gaggle of fascinated kids began to gather around, eager to gawp at their fallen comrade.

"Miss, what's happened?" asked a tall, freckled girl from one of the older classes. "Is he going to die?"

"No, he isn't, Angie, now run to the office and tell them to call an ambulance. And get Miss Laing while you are about it, she's trained in First Aid."

I moved closer to take another look. I was as curious as the other kids, but not about Terry's fate. I couldn't understand why it seemed like a shocking surprise to them. Hadn't they seen this coming just as I had? Apparently, they hadn't. This was the first time it crossed my mind that perhaps others didn't see the world the way I did.

"Don't worry, Miss," I said, confidently. "The ambulance will be here in a few minutes and he will be fine. He comes back to school with crutches in a few weeks."

When she turned and looked at me, I had a distinct feeling that I had said the wrong thing.

"How did you know this would happen?" she demanded, with a questioning, almost accusatory look in her eyes. It made me feel uncomfortable. I was only five years old, but even at that tender age, I could sense what she was thinking.

There's something not right about this boy.

From that day onwards I knew that my ability to see the future was no common human trait. Miss Morris certainly didn't seem to possess it, nor did any of the other kids. Was it only me? If that was the case, then why? What made me so special?

It would be some years before I figured it all out. In the meantime, I had no idea where my premonitions were coming from or when they would pop into my head. I couldn't see everything, just random snippets here and there.

If you had asked me to stand at the side of the street and tell you the colour of the next car to come along, I would have been no more successful at guessing than the next person.

My flashes of insight were unpredictable and usually focused on significant events, those that you would remember for years afterwards.

I had recalled nothing about Terry and his accident until the day I saw him on the climbing frame. That was the moment that had triggered the memory. Nothing much of note happened in school on a day-to-day basis but his accident was a big deal. Years later, people would still say, "Do you remember that time Terry fell off the climbing frame?"

Sometimes I could foresee events that lay years or even decades in the future. A few weeks after the Terry incident, we had our regular Friday afternoon circle time in the classroom. During these sessions, we all sat cross-legged on the floor and our teacher would initiate a discussion topic.

This week, Miss Laing asked what we wanted to be when we grew up. Lots of kids eagerly stuck up their hands and proclaimed confidently that they were going to be a nurse, an astronaut, or a racing driver. Several said the latter, inspired by the current heroics of the latest British hero, James Hunt, on the racetrack.

When it was my turn, I confidently stated: "I'm going to work in the head office of a major national supermarket chain, marry a girl called Sarah and we're going to have a daughter called Stacey."

This rather odd little speech induced a look from my teacher that was reminiscent of Miss Morris in the playground a few weeks earlier. Before Miss Laing could respond, Gary Roper, a hefty kid from one of the rough estates who was already establishing himself as the class bully, chipped in with "Thomas wants to marry the fat girl!"

This brought peals of laughter from the rest of the class, all apart from the girl he was referring to who burst into tears. I had forgotten that we had a girl named Sarah in our class when I made my bold declaration about my future marriage prospects. When Gary had referred to her as the fat girl, he hadn't been exaggerating because she was very overweight.

This was during an era before Britain's childhood obesity crisis kicked in. Back in the 1970s, fat kids were rare which made them stand out from the crowd. It made them easy targets in a time when mocking other kids for being different was rife.

It didn't stop with picking on the fat kids. 'Four eyes' was a common term of derision for those with glasses. Casual racism was also rife, directed at the two only non-white pupils in the school.

These included a quiet, withdrawn Chinese girl who was teased, with various references to dishes at the local takeaway, and a West Indian boy who had acquired the nickname 'Chalky' after a black character in a popular ITV sitcom.

Those with any sort of physical disability were referred to as spastics or spanners. One girl who had painful, flaky eczema was referred to as a leper.

It was cruel and I felt that treating people this way was wrong, but the pack mentality of the school thought differently. It was abundantly clear I was the only one who had a problem with it. I later realised this was because I had experienced life in more enlightened times.

I saw no point in attracting unwanted attention, so I said nothing. Maybe my quiet complicity made me just as guilty as the others, I don't know, but I had learned to keep my mouth shut in such situations. My earlier comments had already led to me being sent to a lady who was described by my parents and teachers as a special doctor. I later learned that she was a child psychologist.

She asked me all sorts of questions, including how I had known Terry was going to fall from the climbing frame. I was wary about exactly where this was leading and just fudged an answer. I said I could see what he had been doing was dangerous and it was just a coincidence that I had predicted his fall.

I deliberately gave dumb or false answers to the rest of her questions, then, after about an hour, she brought the session to a close. I was asked to leave the room while my parents, looking concerned, went in.

When they emerged, there was palpable relief on both of their faces. I knew then that I had done the right thing and was off the hook. I just needed to be careful from that point onwards not to blurt out any more incriminating predictions about the future.

As the next few years went by, I began to understand more about my condition. Before long I was convinced that I was unique. I confirmed this hypothesis by having guarded conversations with my friends where I chose my words carefully. I would ask questions that would inspire predictions that would determine what, if anything, they knew about future events.

For example, I once asked what year they thought humans would first visit Mars. It was the late 1970s at the time and the moon landings were still relatively recent. The predictions varied but most claimed it would be by "The Year 2000."

This was a milestone frequently referred to by people making bold predictions of the amazingly futuristic world we would be living in by then, full of flying cars and robots. I knew that these predictions were impossibly optimistic.

I knew that we had never reached Mars in my lifetime, which ran until at least the 2020s. That seemed to be about as far into the future as I could see. Other questions I asked confirmed what I had already concluded.

None of them knew anything about the future. Sure, they made the occasional correct prediction, but not with any degree of consistency. I just put these down to random lucky guesses, which anyone could make from time to time.

Sometimes visions of my future would present themselves in my dreams. On other occasions, they would be triggered by specific events or encounters, such as the day we went on a family outing to Birdland in Bourton-on-the-Water. I had never been to this pretty, Cotswold village before but as soon I saw the place, I recognised it. I also recalled that there was going to be a massive thunderstorm that afternoon.

I had worked out by now that I had seen this before, not in this life, but another. The memory only came to me when we arrived. It had taken the visual stimulus of seeing the location to trigger my sense of déjà vu.

As predicted, it bucketed down that afternoon and we ended up hiding from the storm in the tropical birdhouse, listening to the rain hammering down on the clear, plastic roof like an endless shower of nuts and bolts. Obviously, I had kept all this to myself. I had no desire to be hauled off to the child psychologist again.

There was a children's show on ITV around this time called *The Tomorrow People* about a group of kids with special abilities. I likened myself to them and wondered if there might be others like me, but if there were, I had no idea of how to find them.

I didn't understand it all yet, but like that day at Birdland, I knew they weren't just visions. I had genuinely experienced these moments before. The question was, how? Had I been reincarnated in some way?

Sometimes my insights only came to me shortly before they happened, but other times I had visions of events far in the future. When I had revealed in class that I was going to marry a woman called Sarah, I wasn't talking about my much-maligned classmate.

I was talking about another Sarah, my soulmate, decades in my future. I knew that I had already shared my life with her, and possibly more than once.

They were mostly happy memories at first, until one night when I woke up sweating and terrified after a truly graphic nightmare. I had seen the image of Sarah's lifeless body lying cold and dead on a slab in a morgue. I was there to undertake the grisly task of identifying her corpse after she had been killed in a road traffic accident.

The shock of the premonition of her death was incredibly traumatic for me to deal with at just seven years old. Then, curiously, the following night, I had another dream that directly contradicted the first one.

This time it was about the events of the day leading up to her death. It gave me foreknowledge of exactly how she was going to die. In the dream, I was able to save her by preventing the drunk driver who had mown her down from driving away from the pub.

It seemed there were two possible futures for Sarah, and I had seen the outcome of each. They couldn't both be true, could they? Either way, I had been given the knowledge I needed to ensure that when the time came, I would know what to do. It was in a future that seemed impossibly far away, but it gave me a sense of purpose. I had my destiny to fulfil.

As always, I kept these dreams to myself, even though I woke up so traumatised by the first one that my instinct was to run to my mother for comfort. I didn't though, and cried myself back to sleep, alone. I knew that talking about the future with my parents would only invite trouble.

However, there were times when I was able to make use of my premonitions without drawing undue attention to myself if I was careful.

It was a family tradition in our house that everyone was allowed a bet on the Grand National, including myself. I soon discovered that every year, on the day of the race, the name of the winner leapt out at me from the paper.

When I suggested, in 1978, that Lucius might do the trick, my Dad put 10p each way on for me at the local bookies, netting me the princely sum of £1.95.

When he paid me the money, he lectured me on the dangers of gambling and that this annual flutter should be seen purely as a bit of fun. Dangerous for others maybe, but not someone who had the sort of edge I did. It was a gift that other gamblers could only dream of.

I didn't want to appear unfeasibly lucky so the following year I deliberately picked a loser. It seemed that I already knew rather a lot about horse racing because I instinctively understood how to read the racecards and what all the different numbers and letters meant. Perhaps it had been a hobby of mine in another life. I could also picture myself at many of the racecourses that they showed on TV, even though in this life I had not yet been to one.

As I grew older, turning eleven in my final year of primary school, my brain continued to mature enabling me to make more sense of the never-ending jumble of memories that flooded into my mind every single day.

I began to sort them into two different categories – long-term and short-term. The former included an increasing number of visions of my life as a husband and a father. Sarah and I had just the one child, Stacey, and I could picture her at all ages from infancy to adulthood.

Several landmark moments stood out. I recalled many special days from her school nativity to her graduation. Many of the memories were from family holidays, such as building sandcastles and jumping over waves in the sea.

These long-term visions mostly came at night. Hardly a night went by that I didn't dream about my future wife and daughter. Unlike other dreams, they didn't fade on waking, the images remaining etched on my mind.

I could picture Sarah as clearly as if I were looking at a photograph, her long, blonde hair framing her pale complexion. I could hear her voice, too, finding the distinctive musical lilt of her South Wales accent appealing and reassuring. I did not doubt that she was a real person who existed in my future and that one day we would be together.

My short-term memories popped up during my waking hours, usually stimulated by some event or other. These premonitions were often invaluable on a day-to-day basis, enabling me to dodge all manner of potential banana skins.

For example, my best friend Martin was heavily into anything to do with astronomy. He had said he wanted to be an astronaut during that circle time session a few years before.

Recently, Martin's parents had bought him a telescope for his eleventh birthday. When he suggested we set it up outside the front of his house to look at the moon, I agreed. As soon as we got outside, on what was a notably frosty, November night, scenes of what might occur during the evening poured into my head.

I recalled that when we had done this before, Martin had thought it would be a bit of a laugh to spy on the neighbours through their bedroom windows. He was particularly interested in an attractive young lady in the house opposite.

He reliably informed me that he was able to ogle at her through a gap in her curtains some evenings as she got out of the shower. He could make out her general body shape from his bedroom window, but that wasn't enough to satisfy his curiosity. He wanted to use the telescope to see what her lady bits looked like close-up.

As soon as he made this dubious suggestion, the recollection of being apprehended by the police and frogmarched home in disgrace flooded through me. I could almost feel the red, raw sting on my buttocks where my father had given me a good hiding afterwards.

One of Martin's neighbours must have seen us and reported us, so I suggested that we set the telescope up in his back garden instead, away from the streetlights where we would get a better view of the moon. Thus, acquiring the unwelcome future nickname, Peeping Tom, was avoided.

I didn't understand Martin's obsession with the female body at that time. My interest in such things didn't develop until I reached my teens and hit puberty, but Martin used to talk incessantly about women and sex all the time, even though his knowledge was somewhat inaccurate. It was based largely on playground hearsay.

On another occasion, the summer following the telescope incident, we stumbled across an old Fine Fare carrier bag filled with dirty magazines under a bush in the park.

Looking inside, I felt quite sickened by some of the pictures of men with large moustaches and sunglasses doing rude things to various naked ladies.

It was the first time I had seen such things in this lifetime. However, I instinctively knew that not only had I seen things like this in my previous life, but I had also done the things in the pictures. Without the moustache and sunglasses, thankfully.

Martin flicked to the centre of one of the magazines where there were two women doing things to each other with strange, rubber objects. There was some accompanying text, but it was in a foreign language which at a guess was probably Dutch or German.

I really didn't want to see any more and urged Martin to throw the bag back in the bush as it wasn't the sort of thing that kids our age ought to be looking at. He laughed and said I must be gay if I didn't like looking at naked women. He promptly stuffed his newly acquired porn stash in his schoolbag and took it home.

A couple of years later, my teenage hormones kicked in and almost overnight girls went from being irritating to irresistible. As my interest in them grew, more images of intimate encounters in lives I had lived before began to flood my mind, and not just with Sarah.

I continued to use my short-term insights to my advantage by ensuring I chose the right fork in the road at every opportunity. One afternoon, I got a strong sense that I should avoid going down to the park after school to play football. I sensed that if I did, Gary Roper, now with the fearsome reputation of being the hardest kid in the school, would end up beating the crap out of me.

I couldn't remember the exact details of why he had done it, only a vague memory of a dispute over whether a goal had only hit the 'post', which wasn't a post at all, just a large pile of coats.

I heeded the warning and stayed home and heard the next day that another kid had been beaten up instead. What the long-term implications of using this information to my advantage might be I hadn't thought about before. Now, after causing someone else to get hurt, I began to have concerns that my actions might be altering the future. That might not be a good thing, even if it was of benefit to me.

I sought answers in the library where I eagerly devoured every science fiction novel I could find, particularly those with themes of time travel or parallel universes. Books such as *The Time Machine*, by H.G. Wells, gave me great insights into the implications of tinkering with the timeline.

There was plenty on TV to get me thinking as well. In the early 1980s, I was watching Peter Davison in *Doctor Who* on weekday evenings and becoming a huge *Star Trek* fan as well. Several episodes which dealt with the subject of time travel related to my situation.

There was one overriding message that was consistent across all these books and TV shows which was that changing history was bad. But to me, this wasn't history. I was rewriting events in future, not the past. I might be able to see two possible outcomes, but no-one else could so what did any of it matter?

By the time I reached my sixteenth birthday in 1986, I had pretty much got it all figured out.

I was seeing two different timelines. The first I had dubbed the 'original' timeline, which I had concluded was from my first life. That was the world in which Sarah had died.

Then there was a second timeline where I had been able to change things with the benefit of hindsight. That's the world in which I had prevented her from being killed.

This second life had come with some unusual properties. I had this overwhelming sense that I had lived it backwards in some way, travelling through my own life getting younger as I went.

By that, I don't mean like in the science fiction story, *The Curious Case of Benjamin Button*, which I had recently read. In that story, the main protagonist had a strange medical condition where he was born old and got younger as the years passed but there was no time travel element involved.

In my second life, I had been getting younger, moving backwards through the years, one day at a time. That was what had enabled me to save Sarah, amongst other things.

I referred to that life as my 'backwards' timeline.

Now I was on my third life, moving forwards again, armed with the various bits of information I could pull together from my two previous incarnations. I needed to decide now what use I ought to be making of this knowledge. What might the consequences be if I didn't use it carefully?

I had already used it to my advantage, such as escaping Gary Roper's clutches and avoiding the incident with Martin and his telescope. These small changes didn't seem to have altered anything important, but what if I carried on doing it?

During my backwards life, I could see that there had been no consequences for anything I did. Each day I had jumped back in time to a point before whatever I had done had happened.

I'm ashamed to admit from some of the sordid memories that came to mind, that I had abused that freedom in ways I wasn't particularly proud of. I had sought out cheap thrills with ladies of dubious virtue and acquired ill-gotten gains from gambling on races when I knew the results in advance.

Most of this had happened in the years after Sarah had been killed. I was lonely and had no opportunity to establish any sort of relationship with a woman due to the weird backwards nature of my existence.

Thinking about some of these unsavoury antics now made me feel dirty but I could erase that possible future simply by ensuring that when the time came, Sarah didn't die. I would not become the shallow, broken person I had been after her death, gambling, whoring, drinking, and smoking myself into an early grave.

Everything revolved around Sarah and Stacey. I had to ensure I kept them safe, and I knew they were both at risk. Not only did I have to prevent Sarah's death, but I also had to protect Stacey. I had begun having disturbing dreams about her suffering a terrifying rape ordeal during her teens.

I didn't know the precise details of when and where it would occur, but experience had taught me that the nearer an event got, the more I tended to remember about it so perhaps the details would be filled in when the time came.

The more I thought about Sarah and Stacey the more I longed to be with them, but they were desperately far away in my future. It was only 1986 and I wouldn't even meet Sarah for another twelve years. Then one day I was hit with a sobering thought. What if our first meeting never took place?

What if the changes I had already made were spreading outwards like ripples on a pond? What if they led to a world where Sarah and I would not end up together?

It was hard to see how relatively minor things like those I had done so far could impact things Sarah was doing hundreds of miles away in South Wales. But I had no experience of exactly how this all worked. The recently released *Back to the Future* movie, which I went to see three times, had done nothing to assuage these fears.

I concluded that it was vital I didn't do anything from this point onwards that might jeopardise the chances of Sarah and I being together in the future. At one point, I wondered whether I ought to risk waiting twelve years at all. She was alive, down in Swansea, why not just go down and find her, right now? Then I wouldn't have to worry about the timeline.

Every part of me ached to be with her but after giving it a lot of thought, I knew that I could not act on these desires. It wasn't the right time. We were not yet the people we would be in twelve years. Trying to make it work now could go wrong for all manner of reasons.

We might not be mature enough for a serious relationship. We lived too far apart, and we had college and careers to pursue before we'd be ready for each other. Plus, there would be other girlfriends and boyfriends we needed to be with first.

All these experiences, good or bad, would shape us into the people we would become. We simply weren't the finished articles yet.

Even if it did work, what if that led to us having another child earlier than we did before? That baby might not be Stacey. It might not even be a girl. How would I feel about that? Would I be able to love another child quite the same way, knowing he or she wasn't quite the same person she should have been?

There was only one possible course of action. I had to be patient and live out those twelve years as closely as possible to my original timeline. That meant resisting the temptation to tamper with events, even if my inaction led me into situations I'd rather avoid.

I would live my life to the letter exactly as I had the first time. I would keep my head down, keep out of trouble and keep my fingers crossed that Sarah would be waiting for me in Ibiza in 1998. Once we were together, and Stacey was born, maybe I could relax that policy, but until then, I must do my utmost to change nothing.

It seemed like a valid plan, and indeed it would have been, except it had one critical flaw that I hadn't taken into consideration. I had confidently assumed that I was the only person in the world with exclusive knowledge of the future.

As I was shortly to discover, I was not.

Chapter Two - Ben

I blame Charlotte for everything.

I had my life all planned out before she came along and ruined it. Now she's turned my kids against me and forced me out of the marital home, yet everyone's taking her side in the divorce.

She's twisted things to the extent that even people I thought were my closest friends now think I'm a twat. That's not me being paranoid. It isn't just a case of being unfriended on Facebook. Some have even had the gall to say it to my face.

It is said that there are two sides to every story. No-one in my daily life will give me the time of day to listen to mine so I've gone down the pub to see if I can garner some support there. Right now, I'm sitting on a barstool and drowning my sorrows in The Red Lion, telling my sorry tale to anyone who will listen.

It's the first time I've set foot in this dump for years and I can see why. It's full of losers. I prefer to frequent more upmarket watering holes, but desperate times call for desperate measures. If I can find just one person amongst this ragtag bunch of lost souls who doesn't think I'm a twat then I'll feel vindicated.

I'm not the sort of person who normally seeks self-validation in this way, but I've got to get it all off my chest.

Even if they end up thinking I'm just another loser like them, I don't care. I know that I'm way better than them.

I've been telling the regulars around the bar all about how I met my wife, in 1988, when I was just eighteen. It's 2020 now so that's well over three decades ago, getting on for half a lifetime. It's wasted time that I will never get back because for most of that time I was utterly bored.

Most men would have jumped ship long ago, but I stuck with her out of loyalty and a duty to our children. Nobody seems to give me any credit for that, not going by the reactions of our family and friends. As for my two daughters, they aren't even speaking to me anymore.

I don't think I was a bad husband. I put food on the table and paid for us to go on holiday every year. We couldn't afford much – a wet week in Tenby if we were lucky, but that wasn't my fault. If I'd gone to university as planned, I'd have had a glittering career and we'd have been jetting off to the Caribbean every year. But I've got her to thank for putting a stop to that.

What went wrong? The silly cow only went and got herself pregnant, that's what. I told her to get rid of it – we were still teenagers, for crying out loud, but no, she had this big anti-abortion thing going on and refused.

She was always banging on about some issue or other. I should have realised the first day I met her when she was wearing a Smiths *Meat is Murder* t-shirt that she was going to be that type. You know the ones, jumping on whatever trendy bandwagon is flavour of the month.

After she found out she was pregnant she tried to blame me for refusing to wear condoms, not that she had been that bothered about it in the heat of the moment.

I had only worn one once before when I lost my virginity to a posh, horsey girl called Rosie West. It was the summer of '87 and we were drunk on cheap cider at a Young Farmers' party just outside Chesterton.

She was a year or two older than me and when she invited me up to the hayloft, it didn't take much persuasion for me to succumb to her advances.

Safe sex was a big deal at the time with the massive AIDS scare striking fear into the populace. Everywhere you looked, from billboards to TV, the 'don't die of ignorance' message was being rammed down your throat.

Rosie insisted on me rubbering up and fortunately she had brought her own because I didn't have any. Afterwards, I felt a bit sore down there and concluded that I must be allergic to latex. I decided that I had better not risk wearing one again and besides, I hated the whole idea of using them anyway. It just didn't seem natural to me.

In my opinion, the whole AIDS thing was being way overblown, but it seemed I was in a minority with that view. When the topic came up in conversation one day in the refectory at college, I said I didn't see what the big deal was.

Most of my friends were horrified, saying that I was being totally irresponsible. When I retorted by saying that I considered contraception to be a woman's responsibility I got called a male chauvinist pig – by a woman, of course. After that, I avoided mentioning the subject again. You know how touchy they can be.

When I met Charlotte and spun her my allergy story, she believed me. I'm sure she said she was on the pill anyway, so it didn't matter. Of course, after she found out she was pregnant, she denied she had ever said anything of the sort, pushing the blame on to me.

We were both drunk at the time which lowered inhibitions so it's all a bit of a blur as to what exactly what was said. I tried to blame it on the drink when it all blew up but got short shrift from the moralistic do-gooders. Apparently, blaming alcohol wasn't an acceptable excuse, even if twentieth-century culture was steeped in booze.

It all happened one drunken lunchtime in early 1988. I was in the second year of a BTEC in Business Studies at a sixth form college in Oxford. It was going well enough for me to have a real prospect of getting into a decent university. I was working hard but enjoyed plenty of leisure time too. Every lunchtime I could be found at the pub opposite the college which was the hub of the student social life.

The Duke was a real old-fashioned, spit-and-sawdust boozer, with cheap beer and an ageing landlord nearing retirement. Old Arthur, who reminded me of the racing pundit John McCririck with his large whiskers and flamboyant clothing, was more than happy to risk serving underage students to boost his pension.

He was certainly doing a roaring trade because the pub was packed every lunchtime. For many, it was an infinitely more attractive option than the library, even if it wasn't doing their livers or their grades any good.

I was young enough to be still enjoying the novelty factor of drinking in pubs and was often eagerly waiting for the front door to open at 11am. My course only involved about twelve hours of lectures a week and most of these were conveniently scheduled outside lunchtime drinking hours.

It was fortunate that pubs hadn't yet started opening all day because I doubt that some of us would ever have gone back after lunch. As it was, I frequently attended afternoon classes somewhat the worse for drink, not that the lecturers ever noticed. Many of them were similarly inebriated after boozy sessions in The Albion, a smoky den of iniquity up the road.

It seems like a different world now, but that was the Britain of the 1980s when boozy lunches were part of the culture, and smoking was allowed pretty much everywhere. Despite this, the economy wasn't suffering. By 1988, Britain was booming with a new breed of affluent, successful youngsters emerging. The media referred to these people as yuppies.

These upwardly mobile types weren't to be found sipping halves of Harp lager and smoking Silk Cut in the back room of The Duke. They were portrayed by the media as champagne-swilling, stockbroker types, consulting their Filofaxes, listening to Dire Straits, and getting rich in the city of London.

It was a lifestyle I aspired to and the main driver behind my choice of business studies. I saw this as my first step towards joining the yuppies. It was all very well hanging around with the plebs in The Duke for the moment, but I knew I was destined for bigger and better things.

I hadn't had the advantage of attending one of the city's top private schools, but I knew plenty who had through my local rugby club. But that didn't matter. In the future, when people asked where I was educated, I could just say Oxford. I didn't need to specify exactly where. The name of the city was prestigious enough.

The A-level students at the college were bearable, but the day-release students, some of whom worked in factories, were very boorish. Thankfully, they were only around one day a week before they went back to whatever mundane, manual job their lowly aspirations had led them to choose.

I made sure I worked hard on my course work in the evenings to make up for any lost time in the pub during the day. I was well ahead of most of my peers, and I made sure they knew it, showing them up with my clever comments in my lectures.

Unfortunately, I had become lumbered with Charlotte. I rue to this day the events that led up to me ending up with her.

It all came down to something as random as a bingo ball being drawn out of a bag. Allow me to explain further.

One of the lads in the pub had come up with the wheeze of running a drinking competition on Friday lunchtimes. It was loosely based around the FA Cup, and I had been drawn against Charlotte in the second round.

I'd only been vaguely aware of her existence before the day of the match. On that afternoon, the large millstone that I would end up carrying around for the next thirty-odd years would be placed around my neck.

Jason, the organiser of the competition, was a larger-than-life character who was always doing this sort of thing. He had already run the pub pool championships and an elaborate killer darts competition in the autumn term. He seemed to get on very well with Arthur who no doubt appreciated all the trade he was bringing into the pub.

He had all his competitions written down in a red Woolworth's exercise book. It contained all manner of complicated stats and league tables and he was forever poring over it. When he approached me while I was playing on the fruit machine and asked if I'd like to take part in his FA Cup of drinking, I thought, why not?

This epic event was scheduled to run throughout the term culminating in a grand final in March.

There was much excitement on the second Friday of term when the draw for the first round took place. Jason had acquired a bag of bingo balls from somewhere and gone to great lengths to arrange an elaborate ceremony like the cup draws I had seen on TV.

It seemed most of the college had turned up for the proceedings and Arthur was doing a roaring trade. The draw was scheduled to take place directly after the traditional lunchtime broadcast of *Neighbours* in the pool room.

Nearly everyone was excited about the competition, apart from one or two killjoys. They believed that encouraging teenagers to drink heavily when they should be studying was in some way irresponsible. Fortunately, they were outnumbered and ignored so the draw went ahead as planned.

The actual first round wasn't scheduled to take place until the following Friday, it was only the draw we had come to see that first day, which Jason seemed more excited about than the competition itself. Early the following week all the participants got a printed sheet with the draw and a list of complex rules.

The basic premise was that each participant scored a goal for each unit of alcohol they drank so a pint was two goals, and a single shot of spirits was one goal.

My tactics were quite straightforward. I would just drink until my opponent ran out of money. We lived in a nice house in one of the villages just outside Oxford and were better off than most of the other students. Many of them lived on council estates and had to do crappy part-time jobs to get their beer money. In contrast, I got a generous allowance from my father at the start of each term.

The first match was easy, just as I expected. I played against Shaun, a BTEC Travel & Tourism student who had ripped jeans and a Manchester accent long before both became fashionable. He wasn't a trendsetter; he was just a poor northern person who couldn't afford a new pair of jeans.

He also only had enough money for half a pint of the pub's cheapest beer, some revolting looking, dark concoction called mild, which I had never seen anyone order before. Apparently, it was popular where he came from.

I did the bare minimum to beat him, having just a pint, winning the fixture 2-1. I made sure that my pint was of the pub's most expensive premium lager, just to hammer home the cultural divide between us. That morning I had been reading in the library's copy of *The Financial Times* about the north/south divide. It was enormous fun gleefully rubbing it in this guy's face while making cracks about flat caps and whippets.

The sixteen students who had made it through to the second round were again allocated numbers to be drawn out of the bag and it was then that fate played its part. The following week I was to be playing against Charlotte.

She was one of three goths who always sat at the table closest to the jukebox, constantly filling the pub with the sounds of The Mission and The Sisters of Mercy. Her whole look was monotone – her pale, white face make-up contrasting with her black, straight, shoulder-length hair.

I used to hang out with two guys from my course, Adam and Mark who liked playing on the fruit machines. The three of us frequently took the piss out of the goths behind their backs, laughing at their clothes, make-up, and depressing choice of tunes on the jukebox.

We never made any attempt to engage them in conversation – why would we? They were clearly into different music and fashions to us. It's not easy to start a conversation with a girl whose favourite choice of tune on the jukebox is a song cheerily entitled *Girlfriend in a Coma*. They gave off an aloof and unapproachable aura most of the time anyway, so we kept our distance.

I was expected to win my drinking match easily against her, according to Jason. He was now offering odds on the matches and made me a hot favourite which was understandable. She was just a girl, after all, and probably half my weight. Her thin and waif-like frame, not much over five feet in height, certainly didn't look capable of soaking up much alcohol.

She didn't have a lot of form either. The results that Jason had issued from the previous week showed that she won her match 1-0 after her opponent had failed to turn up. I was a dead cert to book my place in the quarter-finals.

It was, therefore, a surprise when on the day of the match she marched straight up to me at the bar, looked me up and down and announced, "I'm going to kick your arse!" before ordering a double Bacardi and Coke.

As she finished speaking, 'This Corrosion' by The Sisters of Mercy began to blast out of the jukebox, accompanied by a cheer from her usually subdued gothic friends. I had never seen them so lively.

Adam and Mark started laughing, enjoying my discomfort. It looked like I might be in for more of a battle than I had envisaged.

"Ben's going to get beaten by a girl," said Adam, who never missed an opportunity to take the piss out of people. But his mockery wasn't usually aimed in my direction. He wouldn't dare.

Charlotte turned back from the bar, looked me in the eye, and downed her drink in one. It seemed I had underestimated her, and I needed to think about my drinking strategy if I was going to put this presumptuous girl in her place.

I wasn't much one for drinking spirits but knew I'd never be able to outscore her if I stuck to the beer. I went straight to the bar and matched her order. She promptly ordered another.

An hour later we'd both had six doubles and Arthur was still cheerfully dispensing them without batting an eyelid. Charlotte seemed to be knocking them back effortlessly, but I was feeling distinctly queasy. Although there were several other matches taking place, none had caught fire as ours had and we had acquired a crowd of onlookers.

Charlotte seemed to be revelling at her moment in the limelight and was lapping up the attention. Who would have thought this normally quiet girl, practically invisible as she sat in the corner by the jukebox could suddenly burst into life like this? And why today, of all days?

She downed another double, to another cheer from the crowd who all seemed to be on her side. Then she excused herself to head off to the toilet, giving me the chance to try and drum up some support. All of this wasn't doing my reputation any good at all.

"Don't you worry. I'm not going to get beaten by some girl, especially a goth! I'll show her."

It was at this point that some arsehole wearing a Blues Brothers t-shirt decided to stick his oar in.

"Do you know how misogynistic you sound?" asked the slim built lad I had barely noticed up until this point. He immediately got my back up.

"Ooh look at you with the big words," I replied. "What's it got to do with you? You're not even in this competition, are you?"

"The name's Thomas," he replied. "You don't know what misogynistic means, do you? Well, I suggest you go and find out because if you keep going around talking about women the way you do, you're setting yourself up for a whole lot of trouble in the future. Now show some respect, you're a disgrace."

I was bristling at this guy's audacity, and feeling about ready to punch him, when I felt a tap on my shoulder. I swung round to see Charlotte, freshly returned from the ladies, getting rather up close and personal.

"You know, I really want to win this match," she said. "I think you should let me."

And then she leant forward and whispered in my ear. "I'll make it worth your while." Then, she grabbed me and kissed me full on the lips, inducing a gasp from the crowd. At the same time, unseen by the others she slipped her hand between us and gave me a brief squeeze in the crotch.

I assumed she hadn't heard my conversation with Thomas while she was in the ladies or had only caught the tail end of it. Either way, it didn't matter. It looked like I had pulled without even trying, so Thomas was talking out of his arse.

What was it he had called me – misogynistic? He was right – I didn't know what that meant, but I assumed it meant sexist or something like that. He was just as bad as that chick in the canteen who had called me a chauvinist, but you get these feminists everywhere. I hadn't expected to hear it from a bloke.

He probably fancied himself as one of these new sensitive men I had been hearing about, coming out with a load of feminist claptrap to impress the chicks. I had seen some right-on new comedians spouting similar rubbish on *Saturday Live*. But the joke was on Thomas because who had pulled? Me or him? I rest my case. It looked like the birds preferred real men after all.

I broke away from Charlotte's kiss and looked across at Thomas with a look of triumph on my face that said it all. *I've pulled so screw you.*

I wanted to say it out loud, but I didn't want to risk messing up things with Charlotte. It didn't matter that I wasn't into goths or that I didn't like her T-shirt spouting vegetarian propaganda.

All that mattered was that she was handing herself to me on a plate and it would be foolish to miss an open goal when the offer of sex was on the table. Once I'd had her, it wouldn't matter. I might even let her win the drinking match if it helped me get laid.

When I saw the disgusted look on Thomas's face it only made the moment all the sweeter.

"I'm going to get another drink," said Charlotte. "Which is going to make it 14-12 to me. Then you're going to concede, and I'll show you what this unlocks – in more ways than one."

She reached into her pocket and pulled out a small Yale key.

That was it, I was definitely going to let her win. I couldn't care less about the loss of face of losing to a girl when I was about to get my dick wet. Not long afterwards, the two of us were staggering back across the car park in the middle of a snow shower. Charlotte was clutching the key in her right hand and pulling me along firmly with the other.

"What does this key unlock?" I enquired, as we pushed open the swing doors that led into the main building and a welcome blast of warm air.

"My knickers" she stated, laughing, drunkenly. "And also, this lock." We had turned right down the corridor that led to the library and now she had stopped outside a door I had never taken any notice of before marked, 'Student Union Office'.

"I'm one of the reps," she slurred, drunkenly, before adding, "This key comes with the job."

She was full of surprises. I would never have pegged her as a union rep. I didn't have a lot of time for unions. My grandfather, who was a staunch Tory, reckoned they had ruined the country in the 1970s and I agreed. However, political affiliations were far in the back of mind at that moment. The prospect of imminent sex took priority.

She unlocked the door, practically shoved me in, locked it again behind us and leapt on me like the world was about to end. Things got heated very quickly, the only brief pause in proceedings coming when she asked me if I had a condom. That's when I told her about my latex allergy, and she said it was ok because she was on the pill. That's what I think she said, anyway.

I won't go into details except to say that it was frantic, drunken, and incredibly exciting sex, the likes of which put my previous encounter with Rosie in the shade. I had no idea what I had done to deserve this experience, but at that moment I felt like the luckiest man in the world.

Thirty-two years on I realise that I was, in fact, the unluckiest. I have come to curse that day because it was the day my freedom ended, seemingly forever.

Although my initial intention had been to dump her as soon as I had fucked her, the experience was so amazing that I wanted more. We drifted into a relationship even though I didn't find her particularly interesting as a person. She was always banging on about dreary goth bands I couldn't stand and dragging me down to The Dolly or The Jericho Tavern to watch them.

If I had had any sense, I would have ditched her, but I was eighteen and addicted to the sex, which remained fabulous and a far cry from the joyless, emotionless shagging we would slip into after a few years.

It was different back in 1988 when she was still enthusiastic and adventurous in the sack. There were other considerations too. If I split up with her, there was no guarantee I'd be able to get a shag off anyone else. I'd had over six months without a sniff after that first encounter with Rosie until Charlotte came along. I didn't want to risk that again so decided to stick with her until someone better came along.

That plan was soon to be rendered academic. Less than two months after the day of the infamous drinking contest, she announced she was pregnant. It was on the same day I learnt I had gained a place at the London School of Economics, subject to achieving the required grades. It was a place I was destined never to take up.

I pleaded with her to get rid of the baby, threatening to split up with her if she didn't, but it was all to no avail. In her eyes, abortion was wrong, and that was the end of the argument.

If I expected any support from my close family, I could forget it. Both my father and my mother took me to task over it and told me I had to stand by her. Somehow, at the ridiculously young age of eighteen, I found myself practically frogmarched up the aisle.

Baby Siouxsie came along before the end of the year. It was a ridiculous name in my opinion, but Charlotte insisted on it. She was followed by Julianne, born in 1990. They proved to be our only two children because, after the second one, Charlotte's sex drive fell through the floor. She also started to get fat. Within a few years, that wild encounter in the student union office was a distant memory.

I never made it to the London School of Economics, instead, I became a trainee estate agent. This was something I was duped into believing was the road to riches after the house market boom of the late 1980s. That soon went tits up. By the early 1990s, there was a price crash. The housing market went into freefall and with it went my job.

The spectre of unemployment loomed just at the wrong time as the country fell into recession. By late 1991 I was stacking shelves in Tesco, the only job I could get. It was humiliating and just about as far from my yuppie ambitions as you could get.

I tried other jobs in the years that followed but always seemed to find myself in the wrong place at the wrong time. I got a decent sales job working for Rumbelows but that disappeared when the bottom fell out of the TV and video rental market. After that I went to work for a company that made fax machines, just as email and the internet began to take off, rendering them obsolete.

I lurched from one bad job to another. Every company I worked for seemed to take a downturn shortly after I joined which I swear wasn't down to me. It was just bad luck. Not only that, inevitably I found myself working with humourless, thick people.

At one point I managed to get a decent job at Oxford University which I thought was going well. Then, out of the blue, I found myself hauled up in front of the bosses on a sexual harassment charge. I hadn't even done anything, just cracked a few harmless jokes to try and lighten up the miserable bastards I worked with. But apparently, some stupid bitch had taken offence and reported me.

What was wrong with people? No-one seemed to have any sense of humour anymore. It was no wonder when proper comedians like Bernard Manning hadn't been on the telly for years.

It didn't stop there. As I soon discovered, these things follow you around for life. Far more recently, I found out I'd been named and shamed on Twitter by that very woman who had reported me to HR all those years before. She had the audacity to tag me with this #MeToo nonsense, all because I once asked her to photocopy her tits for a laugh at the Christmas party.

My bad luck extended to my investments. I had two decent inheritances in the 2000s and both times decided to invest it all in the stock market. I came badly unstuck on each occasion, first after 9/11 and then again with that whole credit crunch debacle. My investments weren't bad choices. It was all down to the timing.

If my father had lingered on another year or two, I would have got my inheritance in 2009 instead of 2007. Then I would have been laughing, as the stock market was at rock bottom in 2009. But no, the stupid old duffer had to pop his clogs in time for me to invest it all in Northern Rock.

My life has been one long catalogue of disappointment. My marriage is over. Charlotte threw me out after she came home from work early one day and found me in our bed with some slapper I met on Tinder. She went ballistic, bad-mouthed me all over town and trashed me on social media.

Now I'm reduced to renting a room in a shared house and working nights in a 24-hour petrol station. To say my life's a train wreck would be an understatement. It's been a bloody miserable winter for weather as well with constant rain and flooding.

It's March now, and spring is on the way, but all the news is of some new virus sweeping the country. That was all the regulars at the bar were talking about when I came in. Their main concern seemed to be about where they would go if the pubs got forced to close because of it. I could understand their concern as some of them looked as if they spent their entire lives in there. Where would they go?

Under the circumstances, I was surprised they were willing to listen to my sorry tale, but after half an hour of it, they were still paying attention. I was even managing to garner a little sympathy at my plight. Occasionally when I paused, they would chip in with comments on their own similar experiences.

"I had that whole sexual harassment thing with The Met," said the pub's landlord, Richard Kent. He was the ex-chief of the local police. "That's how I ended up in this backwater."

"Tell me about it," I replied, grateful for the support. "My life could have been so different if I hadn't got stuck with that bitch."

"You think you had it bad!" exclaimed Andy, a scruffy, and slightly smelly man dressed in outdated double denim. "I was nearly a huge rock star. Bigger than Jon Bon Jovi I would have been if I hadn't been screwed over. Here, let me tell you all about what happened."

I looked up at Kent who gave me a warning shake of the head that suggested I really wouldn't want to hear it. I needed to go and take a leak, anyway, so now seemed an opportune moment to duck out.

"In a minute, mate, I need to pay a visit first," I said, hopping off the barstool where I had been seated since my arrival in the pub, three pints earlier.

I walked to the back of the pub, straight through the wooden door marked 'Gents' and towards the metal trough into which the pub's drinkers returned the beer they had recently purchased.

There was a condom machine on the wall next to the window on which some joker had crudely scrawled "Buy me and stop one," in permanent, black marker pen. It was hardly an original joke – I had seen it many times over the years including on the machine in The Duke all those years ago.

If only I'd taken notice at the time. Maybe I shouldn't have been so selfish by refusing to wear condoms all these years. Charlotte wouldn't have fallen pregnant for a start.

No, I needed to stop thinking like this. I had to keep telling myself, it wasn't my fault, it was hers. If she hadn't got so drunk that first day and spent the whole evening after we'd had sex throwing up, her contraceptive pill might not have ended up in the toilet. If she had even been taking them in the first place. I still had my doubts about that because I had never seen them at the time.

I could not start feeling bad about myself. As long as I kept blaming everything that had gone wrong in my life on bad luck and other people, then I wouldn't lose my self-esteem. Without that, I would have nothing.

"It's not me, it's them!" I said aloud, reinforcing my beliefs, as I unzipped my trousers. Relieving myself, another man came in and stood next to me.

I didn't look across at him because that would be breaking urinal etiquette. He had no such qualms, going one step further by forgoing the traditional silence to engage me in conversation.

"I couldn't help overhearing you at the bar," began the man. "It sounds like you've had a bit of bad luck there."

"A bit!" I exclaimed. "More like a whole lifetime's worth."

"I bet you wish you could go back in time and do things differently, don't you?" said the man.

I finished, zipped back up, and turned to look at him. He was slightly greying, and I guessed he was about my age. I couldn't recall seeing him in the pub earlier, but I suppose he must have been there. How else would he have heard?

"Who wouldn't?" I replied. "But we only get one shot at life, don't we?"

"Not necessarily," he said. "What if I told you I could send you back in time right now?"

"I'd say you've been watching too many *Black Mirror* episodes, mate."

"Seriously, I can do it," he said, reaching into his jacket pocket and pulling out a metal, wand-like device. "With this."

"Prove it," I said, not taking this seriously at all. The bloke clearly had a screw loose.

"OK, how about that day you were talking about at the bar, in 1988?" he said. "Do you remember the precise date?"

"It's permanently etched on my mind," I replied. "29th January 1988. How could I forget? But please, spare me your crazy fantasies about time travel, you're obviously some sort of weirdo."

"Oh, they aren't fantasies," replied the man. "As it happens, I time travelled here myself from the 2050s."

"And why would you want to do that?" I asked, humouring the idiot. "What's so great about 2020? Unless you're a Liverpool fan or fancy a dose of Coronavirus I can think of plenty of better years to visit than this one."

"This is when I was young, about the age you would have been in 1988," he replied. "You could say I've got a soft spot for this era and the people in it. I like to help them out when I can. It's a bit of a hobby of mine."

"Really? Can't you just get an allotment or play golf like normal middle-aged people? Seriously I've heard enough.

If you really can send me back in time, prove it. Otherwise, I'm going back to the bar for another pint."

"I will," he replied, holding up his weird, metal stick. "I'll just send you back for a day, then I'll whisk you back here and we'll see how you got on."

"Whatever," I replied, not for a moment expecting anything to happen. I knew this pub attracted some weirdoes, but I had no idea they were now letting them out of the local mental homes for a pint."

"Don't you have any questions for me?" he asked. "For example, any tips to help you get the best out of your day in the past?"

"What's the point? You're a deluded fantasist," I replied.

"If you say so," he said, pointing his wand in my direction. "I'm sure you'll have lots of questions when you get back."

Then, remarkably, everything changed. One second, I was throwing a crumpled, blue paper towel in the bin whilst walking towards the door, then suddenly I was waking up in my teenage bedroom in 1988.

Chapter Three - Thomas

By early 1988 I had developed a strong understanding of who I was and who I had been before. What had initially seemed bewildering as a child, now made perfect sense. I was able to stride confidently into adulthood with a sense of purpose.

By now I could identify not only the future significant events in my own life but also many major world events that would play out in the years ahead.

In the here and now, many little reminders continued to pop into my mind during the minutiae of my daily life. These were often only minutes or even seconds before they occurred and invariably played out exactly as I envisaged.

I rarely acted on these instincts unless it was to avoid a particularly unpleasant or dangerous situation. The rest of the time I stuck to my policy of preserving the timeline and as far as I could tell, everything was proceeding according to plan.

I had tried my utmost to do everything of any note exactly as I had before, achieving the right grades in my GCSE's, taking the same subjects at A-Level, and interacting with the same friends at college.

That included girlfriends, even though that left me facing a moral dilemma on more than one occasion. The first time was concerning my first sexual experience. I was on holiday in France, when I met my first love, Simone, an encounter that I remembered from my original life with great affection. Raging with teenage hormones as I had been at the time, I recalled that I was besotted with this girl. I had been heartbroken when I had to return to the UK, knowing I would never see her again.

This time around, the experience felt somewhat different. My heart lay with Sarah in the future and despite my physical attraction to Simone, the romantic feelings from my original life were distinctively devoid of their previous intensity.

I let events play out as they had done, losing my virginity in our holiday caravan in the extreme heat of a Bordeaux August afternoon. Afterwards, I felt strangely detached and more than a little guilty. Was I being disloyal to the future Sarah by still indulging my desires with Simone knowing what I now knew?

I wrestled with these questions alone, as there was no-one I could turn to for moral guidance. My unique situation wasn't the sort of thing that was going to be covered in the problem pages in the tabloids. In the end, I just decided to stick to the plan and do whatever it was I had done before.

When heartfelt love letters, scented with perfume and written on beautiful rose petal paper started arriving from Simone, I dutifully replied, even though my heart wasn't in it. I knew that the letters would fizzle out within a year or two, like many a teenage romance that seemed like the most important thing in the world until the harsh reality of adult life kicked in.

I'm not sure who it was who once said that we are the sum total of our life experiences, but it meant perfect sense to me. Everything I would do over the next decade or so would shape me into the person I would be when Sarah and I met for the first time. I didn't want my personality to deviate from that in any way by taking a different path.

It seemed to be working because the world kept turning as it should. Elections and sporting events came and went, with the results exactly as I anticipated. I resisted the attempt to take advantage, other than allowing myself to win a little most years on the Grand National. I was still relying on my father to put these bets on for me, but I would soon be old enough to get into the betting shop myself.

In the wider world, major news events, often disasters of some kind, continued to happen on schedule. There seemed to be a lot of avoidable catastrophes in the 1980s. I always agonised over these when they took place, thinking about the poor people who had died. Was it morally right of me to allow these things to happen? Could I have stopped them? It could be argued that saving lives was a far less selfless cause than prioritising my own future needs.

I wrestled with these thoughts periodically, particularly after I read a piece in a science journal about the butterfly effect. That suggested that I'd already changed the world countless times because I couldn't ensure I did absolutely everything the same as in my previous life.

Every day I was probably treading on insects that wouldn't have died before because my footsteps wouldn't have been in precisely the same place at the same time. I couldn't replicate my previous life to that level of detail.

Would any of that matter? Did these things make much difference in the grand scheme of things? I understood the whole idea of chaos theory, but it didn't seem to be happening, so perhaps it was just that – a theory.

Maybe over vast, evolutionary timescales, I might make a difference, but it didn't seem to be enough to disrupt the world around me in the short term. Everything went on as it should, which meant I was able to enjoy the good memories all over again.

One of those came on the day when Oxford United won the League Cup, or Milk Cup as it was then known, in 1986. It was their only major trophy.

It was unfortunate that I would have to watch them plummet down the divisions in the years ahead after Robert Maxwell's money dried up and he fell off his yacht. However, I wasn't going to let that spoil my enjoyment of their day in the sun at Wembley.

It was my first visit to the national stadium with the added enjoyment of knowing in advance that we were going to thrash QPR 3-0.

Most of the time I refrained from talking about the future to people due to past problems. However, occasionally I couldn't resist throwing the odd cultural prediction into conversations to show off. I spent the whole of the run-up to the big match telling everyone confidently that Oxford were certain to win.

A lot of people rubbished this, as QPR were favourites, but I was able to enjoy plenty of "told you so" moments afterwards.

I made myself look like an expert on the music scene, by making bold predictions about the bright prospects of up-and-coming bands. To complete the image, I often wandered around with a copy of *Sounds* under my arm.

"Mark my words," I would say. "This T'Pau track has got number one written all over it."

A week or two later I would bask in the satisfaction of being proved right when *China in Your Hand* topped the charts. This gained me considerable kudos from my friends. I didn't think this sort of thing wasn't going to do any harm, and so it proved. Up until early 1988, everything was going swimmingly.

Then, one Friday lunchtime in late January, there was an unexpected development. The most concerning thing about it was that it involved two people with whom I had previously had little interaction. Nothing I had done before could have had any influence over their behaviour on that day.

I was hanging out in The Duke where some of the other students had organised a drinking competition. I wasn't participating myself, not that I wouldn't have enjoyed the opportunity. The only reason I wasn't taking part was that I had been off sick for a few days with a vile cold and had missed the chance to sign up.

Interestingly, I had known the cold was coming, because I remembered that I'd had it in the original timeline. It truly was a horror, coughing and sneezing all over the place and snot pouring out of my nose like the Niagara Falls. The only positive thing I could say about it was that if I had managed to pick up the same virus at the same time as before, then at least the timeline was on track.

I believe I caught it at New Year when we had a family gathering. One of my cousins was suffering from it and was sneezing all over the place. That's not what you want when your parents have put on a buffet. The sausage rolls must have been crawling with germs.

Once I had recovered and was back at college, everyone was talking about this drinking competition. I remembered it being quite rowdy in my original timeline so I went along to the pub to observe what I assumed would be an entertaining spectacle.

It certainly was, and I watched proceedings with amusement right up until the moment when everything veered off-course. Up until that point, there had been nothing at all to suggest anything was deviating from normal.

It all centred around this lad called Ben who was sometimes in the pub at lunchtimes. You'll note that I said lad, not friend, and with good reason. I hadn't seen a lot of him, but what little I had seen had been enough to make me take a sharp dislike to him.

Why didn't I like him? He was a complete loud-mouth for a start. He was always showing off about how much money he had compared to the other students and about his posh house outside Oxford. He also went on all the time about how clever he was and how he was considering offers from various top universities. Then there was all the crap about his yuppie rugby playing friends. It was never-ending.

Then there were his outfits. He dressed ridiculously in a blazer and cashmere jumper that might not have looked out of place in a local prep school but stuck out like a sore thumb amongst the standard student uniform of t-shirt and jeans.

On top of that, he was incredibly prejudiced against women, like some ghastly, outdated character from a 1970s sitcom. Previously, in the pub, I had heard him use phrases like "a woman's place is in the home" and "women are only good for one thing." These things were never said when women were within earshot, of course, only in the company of Adam and Mark, his two lapdogs.

They seemed to look up to him, which only encouraged him. I struggled to understand why people didn't challenge his behaviour, but attitudes were changing and perhaps they would, given time. I knew for certain that Ben's comments simply wouldn't be tolerated in the twenty-first century.

Despite my enjoyment of watching the drinking matches, there was one moment I wasn't looking forward to because it was a prime example of why there was no justice in the world.

I remembered it all in detail and could almost feel my annoyance and frustration from the previous time. Ben had been in a drinking match with Charlotte, a girl from my tutor group I had chatted to a few times.

She seemed level-headed, was studious, and had a great taste in music. I soon remembered feelings that reminded me of the enormous crush I'd had on her in my first life. Unfortunately, my shyness had prevented me from asking her out in that original life, and as per the rules I lived by, she was off-limits in this one.

My failure to act in that original timeline had a cruel sting in the tail. She was not the sort of person I could ever imagine being impressed by the likes of Ben which was what made her behaviour that day so incomprehensible.

You know that thing where you look at a couple and you think, how on earth did they ever get together? This was a prime example.

I watched, fascinated, as they started knocking back double Bacardi's, seeing everything play out before. He grew more boorish with every drink, bragging about how he was going to beat this chick, as he referred to her.

Quite what she found attractive in this, I will never understand, but there must have been something. I knew that in a few minutes, inexplicably, she was going to kiss him, right in the middle of the pub. Then she was going to drag him off somewhere to have sex.

How did I know about the sex? Because Ben couldn't wait to brag about it in the pub the following Monday lunchtime.

After that, I remember little about them, so I assume that they had no further impact on my life. I have a vague feeling that they became a couple but after that nothing. Maybe they dropped out of college. That wasn't unusual – a high percentage of students left their courses for one reason or another.

Perhaps more memories would come to me later. One had come to me right now. I remembered getting involved and giving him a piece of my mind. Recalling what I had said, I waited until she went off to the toilet, and he started mouthing a load of sexist rubbish to his mates. That's when I stopped him and recited my lines, word for word.

After this brief and rather unfriendly exchange, we were interrupted by Charlotte coming back from the toilet. This was the moment when she had decided to kiss Ben. And that was the moment when the timeline lurched dramatically off course.

"Get off me, you slag," he shouted, pushing the shocked girl roughly away. "You must be crazy if you think I'm going to be caught out a second time."

"I'm sorry," she began. "I thought that you…"

"Well, you thought wrong," he said, interrupting her mid-sentence. He turned to face the watching crowd who had been stunned into a horrified, yet fascinated silence by the outburst.

"Listen carefully, lads. Don't touch this one with a bargepole. She'll get herself up the duff, trick you into marriage and then you'll be saddled with her for life. Trust me, I've been there."

"Come on mate, there's no need for that," said Jason, the organiser of the drinking contest, attempting to cool things down. "I think this has got a little out of hand."

"This whole thing was your idea, mate, so it's your fault. Just remember what I said. She might try and get her claws into you next."

"Right, Ben, that's enough," announced the usually quiet and easy-going Arthur from behind the bar. "I think you had better leave."

This was unprecedented. Arthur never threw anyone out, not if they still had money in their pocket.

"Don't worry, old man, I'm going. Back to the life I should have had before this bitch ruined it."

He pointed at Charlotte, who was now beginning to weep under his onslaught. A single tear ran down her white cheek, making her make-up run. This didn't go unnoticed by the crowd. You could almost sense the disapproval towards

Ben amassing in the air, like a vile smell spreading through the room.

"Oh, don't turn on the waterworks," he snapped at her, showing no sympathy whatsoever. "Take no notice, you lot – she always does this."

"Who the fuck do you think you are?" shouted Molly, one of Charlotte's gothic friends who I don't think I had ever heard speak before.

"He's a disgusting, sexist pig, that's who he is," added Lisa, the third goth, who always wore a huge, silver crucifix around her neck.

"Like I care what you think," scoffed Ben.

"Out!" yelled Arthur. "Now! Or I'll throw you out myself."

"I'd like to see you try," replied Ben, arrogantly. "How old are you, anyway? Seventy? Cool it old man, I was already leaving. The sooner I get out of this dump, the better. You two coming?" he asked, turning towards his mates.

"I don't think so," said Adam, nervously.

"No," replied Mark, more firmly. "Lisa's right. We don't want to hang out with you anymore."

"Suit yourself. I don't need you pair of losers anyway. Or any of you in here, come to that. You'll see."

He drained the rest of his rum and coke, slammed the glass down on the cheap, round Formica table and walked out the door.

"Later, losers!" he shouted as a parting shot, as the crowd rallied around Charlotte to offer her support.

I had watched this whole scene play out with a growing sense of dread. Not because of Ben's behaviour, horrific as it was, but because this wasn't what was supposed to happen.

It was unprecedented. Up until now, my memories had painted an accurate picture of what was going to occur each day. So how could the last few minutes have played out so differently?

Was it something I had done? I couldn't see how. I had barely had any interaction with Ben before that day. Sure, I had spoken to him just before Charlotte came back from the toilets, but that was supposed to happen. It can't have been that which triggered the change.

Some of the things he had said during his rant had also set alarm bells ringing. He had gone on about her getting pregnant and ruining his life as if he had foreknowledge of those events. Did he? And if so, why now, and not in my original life?

"Trust me, I've been there," he had said. Those words reverberated around in my head. If he had been there and lived these events in the future, then it would explain why he had acted the way he had. It was vital that I went after him and found out.

Downing my drink, a modest half of lager, I grabbed my coat and slipped out of the pub unnoticed, less than a minute after Ben. I could see him, about fifty yards ahead of me, heading back towards the college.

I shivered, just as a heavy snow shower broke out and quickly pulled my red ski-jacket over my Blues Brothers T-shirt.

"Ben, wait up," I called as I ran after him, my breath billowing out in front of me in the cold, winter air.

He stopped and looked back at me as I ran towards him. Even at a distance, I could make out the sneer on his face. I couldn't imagine he was the easiest person to deal with at the best of times. Right now, he was drunk and angry which was never a good prelude to any conversation.

"Oh, it's you," he said, condescendingly. "Thomas the do-gooder. What do you want? Come to give me a load of feminist claptrap like you did earlier?"

"No, it's nothing like that," I replied. Much as I would have liked to have given him a piece of my mind, there were more important considerations in play.

"I simply want to know why you did what you did just now," I added.

"What's it got to do with you?" he bristled, threateningly. "Why don't you just back the hell off?"

I needed to tread carefully. I was slim and puny compared to him and I didn't fancy my chances if this got out of hand.

"I'm simply curious as to why you rejected Charlotte when she tried to kiss you in the pub. Don't you fancy her?"

I was trying to ask in a way that didn't give him any indication as to my true nature. At least not before I had established his.

"You were there, you heard what I said," he replied. I've no intention of getting snared in her trap a second time. Married with a kid at my age? I don't think so."

"What do you mean by a second time?" I pressed. "It sounds as if you know about future events. Maybe like someone who could time travel. Can you?"

He peered closely at my face, then a look of realisation spread across his as he jumped to a conclusion. It was the wrong conclusion, but at least it moved the conversation in the direction I wanted it to go.

"Oh, I get it," he said. "You're him, aren't you? A younger version come to check up on me. How am I doing?"

"A younger version of who?" I replied, intrigued. I had no idea who he thought I was.

"I don't know your name – we met in the toilets in The Red Lion in 2020 and you sent me back here to 1988."

"I can assure you, that wasn't me. However, I do know a thing or two about time travel," I replied. "Interested?"

Much as I despised Ben, I was willing to put that to one side for the moment. It was vital to find out more about why he had been sent back here. The last thing I needed was anyone else contaminating the timeline.

"Oh, really," he said, scathingly. "Like what?"

He was so aggressive. If the circumstances were different, I'd have called him an arsehole, but this was important. I had to try and be diplomatic.

"You know, Ben, you're not the easiest bloke to deal with, has anyone ever told you that?"

"Don't change the subject, mate," he said. "If you reckon that you're some big expert on time travel then prove it!"

We were still standing in the middle of the car park as the snow continued to fall, and I shivered, even in my thick ski jacket. We needed to take this indoors. I'd tell him the truth, then he would want to know more and would come with me.

"Right, I will," I said firmly. "I came out here after you because I know what's supposed to happen in this timeline. I've seen it all before. You didn't do what you were supposed to in The Duke. In the original timeline, you didn't reject

Charlotte. The two of you snogged in front of everyone and then you went off somewhere. Is this making sense so far?"

"Spot on," he conceded, finally adopting a more reasonable tone. I had got his attention.

"So, what's your story?" he asked.

"I'll explain, but first can we go somewhere warm and talk about this before we catch our death of cold. Preferably not another pub because I think you've had enough, and not the college either. I think you're probably persona non grata around here right now after what happened earlier."

"Doesn't matter," he replied. "By tomorrow none of this will matter."

I wasn't sure what he meant by that but intended to find out.

"Come on then," I said. "I'll buy you a coffee and you can tell me all about it."

"All right, then," he said, softening now there was some common ground between us. "There's a café around the corner, we can go there."

"Perfect," I replied. "I could do with that coffee, and I'm certain you could."

Much as I despised Ben, he was another time traveller. There was no way I was letting him out of my sight until I established exactly how he had ended up here, and more importantly, what his intentions were now that he was here.

"Come on then," he said, and we began to walk up Norfolk Street towards Westgate.

Chapter Four - Ben

That, I had not expected.

One minute I was having a bizarre conversation with some nutter in a pub toilet who offered to send me back in time.

The next I was waking up in 1988, something I would quite happily have laid odds of a million to one against happening. Wouldn't anyone? If some weirdo came up and offered to send you back to 1988, what would you think? You couldn't possibly take it seriously, no matter how much the idea might appeal.

But happen, it had, because unless I had suddenly gone insane, there was no denying where I had ended up. I had done the guy in the pub a disservice calling him a fantasist.

Any initial thoughts that this might be some sort of elaborate confidence trick were soon dispelled. No-one could fake this, the detail in the room was spot on. Everything was exactly where it should be, from the ZX Spectrum on the desk to the topless posters of Linda Lusardi that I had spent many a pleasant teenage moment looking at.

The only other possibility was that I was dreaming, hallucinating, or had been hypnotised in some way. I suppose those things were possible. That guy might have done something to me to make me imagine all this, but how? Not by any technology I had ever heard of. As for dreams, I never questioned them when I was having them, no matter how outlandish. It was only when I woke up that I realised how ludicrous they were.

Scouting around the room added further confirmation. Even the old copies of *Razzle* and *Men Only* with their pages stuck together were in their correct location. I used to hide them at the back of the wardrobe in an old Fresh Fruit Daily carrier bag.

I unpicked the pages and had a flick through, reacquainting myself with a few old friends. I was struck by how much hair women had back then – both up top and down below. Fashions had changed enormously in that area in the intervening years.

Resisting the temptation to knock one out, I put the bag back and rummaged through my clothes. I needed to get going and could easily lose track of time if I spent all day reminiscing over the contents of my room. I had a mission to fulfil.

I didn't need to look through the window to know how cold it was outside. I could see the frost on the pane, and I would need some warm clothes. I picked out one of my favourite tops, a red, cashmere jumper from my extensive collection. I bought them from a posh shop in town and loved wearing them to college. They marked me out as a cut above the rest of the student plebs.

Next, I headed to the bathroom to freshen up. The room was exactly as I recalled. However, I couldn't remember some of the minutiae, such as which toothbrush belonged to me. I couldn't be expected to have retained that level of detail after all this time. I wonder how many toothbrushes the average person gets through during a lifetime. I had never had cause to think about such things before.

I believe that I am significantly cleverer than your average person, but even a brain the size of mine can only retain so much information. It had reasonably concluded that I would no longer need to remember what colour the toothbrush was that I was using thirty-two years ago.

I took the newest looking one, gave it a good rinse and then squeezed some Signal toothpaste on to it. That was a blast from the past. I hadn't seen that brand for years. Did they still make it in my time? I wasn't sure.

Ablutions complete, I returned to my bedroom to finish dressing. I pulled on my blazer, another mark of my social status, and looked in the mirror at my impossibly young features and skinny, chiselled jawline. I was a muscley guy too. That was down to the rugby.

What a handsome young fellow I was! The only thing I wasn't happy about was my hair. What the hell was I thinking of having a haircut in the same style as Bros? It was cringeworthy.

Fully dressed, I left my bedroom and made my way downstairs. I was relieved to discover that both my parents had left for work because I had no desire to talk to them. They were always giving me shit during my teenage years about lack of respect and all that crap. Stupid old twats, what did they know?

After the whole pregnancy debacle, they took every opportunity to remind me what a huge disappointment I had been to them. In the years that followed, we drifted apart, and I can't say I was particularly sad at either of their funerals. All they had done my whole life was disapprove of me.

Once they were both dead, I could do what I wanted. It's just a shame I'd lost the inheritance money on the stock market. If that had worked out differently, it would have been me ditching Charlotte, not the other way around.

Did I want to do anything to try and patch things up with my parents, now I had the chance? The answer was a resounding no. Why reopen old wounds? They weren't going to be any more reasonable now than they had been before. I might have thirty years of hindsight behind me, but they didn't.

Before I left the house, I checked out good, old Ceefax, on the portable colour TV in my room. It confirmed I had come back to the right date. Stepping outside into the bitter January air, I managed to find my way to the bus stop and on to the correct bus to take me into college. It was one of those old-fashioned, red double-deckers. They were like the old, London buses but without the door at the back.

I hated using public transport most of the time because it was always full of annoying people. From the old people who took ages fiddling around with their small change to pay the driver, to the horrible kids, with snot dribbling down their faces who wouldn't stop screaming, it was consistently awful.

But today, I enjoyed the ride into Oxford immensely, ignoring the great unwashed, as I marvelled at just how much had changed over the years.

The bus passed old pubs, long gone, buildings now demolished, and a steady stream of old-fashioned cars. Many of these were made up the road in Cowley by British Leyland. The number plates suggested some of these cars were barely a decade old but already looked like they were falling apart with rust.

The journey didn't take long as we cruised down the bus lane along Botley Road, past disgruntled drivers stuck in a jam. One thing never changed in Oxford and that was the rush hour, which lasted all day.

By the time the bus pulled into Gloucester Green, it wasn't long until The Duke was due to open. I felt almost giddy with the anticipation of what was to come. I had worked out my dastardly plan in the ten minutes I had been sitting on the top deck of the bus.

I felt full of confidence about what lay ahead. It was in my hands to change my destiny and it was the simplest of tasks. All I had to do was reject Charlotte's advances, thus ensuring we never had sex and she never got up the duff. Then I could enjoy the rest of the day before whizzing back to 2020 to enjoy a new, improved life in an altered timeline.

As soon as I arrived in the pub, I looked over to the jukebox where I knew she would be. Sure enough, there she was, one of the three gothic witches, as I used to think of them.

She was so young! I had expected this, obviously, but it was still a shock. I had been so used to living with the lazy, fat lump she had turned into, I had forgotten how gorgeous she had been in her youth.

Remarkably, and worryingly, I felt an unexpected surge of arousal, seeing her as she had once been. This wouldn't do at all. Maybe I should have sorted myself out earlier when I was flicking through my old jazz mags. It would have dampened down my testosterone levels.

I quickly suppressed these sexual thoughts, urging myself to focus on how much she had ruined my life. I was angry at her for making me feel attracted to her again, and now I wanted to punish her for it. It wasn't just a simple rejection she was going to get now. I was going to milk every last drop of satisfaction out of this.

I wanted revenge and I wanted to humiliate her, and I was bloody well going to enjoy it. I didn't give a shit what anyone else thought of me. It wasn't as if I was going to have to spend more than a day around any of these people, anyway. I had long lost touch with all of them.

I found the other students incredibly irritating and immature, even more so than I remembered. This included Adam and Mark, the two lads I used to knock around with at the time. Seeing them again, I couldn't imagine why.

There was also this other arsehole, called Thomas, who tried to give me a lecture about not being sexist. There was enough of that bullshit in the twenty-first century, without having to hear it in this era.

When the moment came, and Charlotte tried to kiss me, I relished every gorgeous second, slagging her off to high heaven in front of the pub. It was like one of those scenes in *Eastenders* when the whole pub is stunned into silence. I went so over the top that I even managed to get kicked out of the pub by the old coffin dodger who ran it.

It had been glorious. Being able to behave disgracefully without fear of consequences was a strange and intoxicating drug. It left me craving more, much more. If only I could do this sort of thing whenever I wanted.

Oh, the scores I could settle with the people who had wronged me down the years! There was that #MeToo bitch for a start, she needed taking down a peg or two. Unfortunately, I had only been offered one day.

After I left the pub, I thought that was the whole Charlotte matter done and dusted. What else could I do? I hadn't really planned beyond my main objective. Before I could ponder any further on that I heard a voice calling me from behind. I realised I had been followed from the pub.

It was that do-gooder, Thomas. What did he want? My first thought was that he had come to give me another of his trendy right-on lectures about my attitudes towards women. In my drunken state, I thought about just punching him in the face and moving on, but then he started talking about time travel. That stopped me right in my tracks. He had sussed me.

Somehow, he knew what I was up to. I had naively assumed no-one would have an inkling – how could they? Yet here he was, saying things that he couldn't possibly know. What was his motivation? Had he come to stop me? If he had, then he was too late. The deed was done.

When he suggested going for a coffee to discuss it, I was wary. I didn't like people like Thomas, and under ordinary circumstances, I would have had no desire to spend any time with him. I wasn't afraid of him in the slightest – not physically anyway. I could have kicked his arse from one end of the car park to the other if I had been so inclined.

I was more concerned with what other powers he might have. If he knew about time travel, then he might possess the ability to undo what I had done. He could even be the man who had sent me here in the first place. He looked completely different but that could be explained. Thomas was a teenager, like me, and the man who sent me here had been middle-aged. How many people can be recognised from their photos of their teenage selves decades later?

Curiosity got the better of me. If I just floated off back to 2020, I'd be wondering evermore. Even worse, I could find myself back in the same pickle as before I left. I may as well hear what he had to say. It was only a coffee after all.

Reluctantly, I agreed and ten minutes later, we found ourselves in the long-defunct Fenwick's café on St Ebbes. It seemed that they had only one type of coffee. Cappuccinos and lattes had not made their way into this old-fashioned place yet.

It was plain, filter coffee, but that was simply fine by me, especially at 40p a cup. I was back in the days before coffee shops realised if they gave their drinks fancy names, they could charge twice as much for them. Ordinarily, money wasn't a problem for me in my youth, but I was a little low on funds today because of the amount of money I had spent in the pub.

As soon as we were seated, Thomas started firing questions at me.

"Right, as I said before, I want to know exactly why you did what you did earlier in the pub. Specifically, why did you reject Charlotte's advances?"

Should I be cagey with him, or just tell the truth? I usually had no hesitation about lying my way out of tricky situations, but today I decided to be honest. If he really was another time traveller, I needed to gain his trust, at least for the time being. Just until I had figured out what his role was in all of this.

"Because I knew what would happen if I didn't. I would have ended up going back to college with her and shagging her in the student union office. Next thing I know, she's pregnant and my life's ruined."

"OK, we've established you knew in advance what would happen," said Thomas. "What I want to know is how?"

"Don't you already know that?" I replied, getting annoyed with his questions. "Aren't you the one who sent me back here in the first place?"

"It wasn't me who sent you back here," he said. "But I knew right away in the pub that you had seen this day before because I have seen it too. That's how I knew that you hadn't done what you were supposed to in the pub."

"What's your story, then?" I asked intrigued. "Were you sent back here from the future too?"

"No, not at all," replied Thomas. "I have no idea who sent you back in time. I'm living a normal life, in my own body, but the strange thing about it is it's not my first. I've lived this life twice already and can recall all sorts of details of days yet to come, ranging from the mundane to major world events."

"Prove it," I challenged him. A few concrete details of his credentials wouldn't go amiss.

"Easy," he replied. "What year did you say you came here from?"

"2020," I replied.

"That's a notable year," he replied. "I've seen visions of it many times. The whole year will be dominated by a new virus called Covid-19 which causes a global pandemic and Donald Trump is president of the USA. Need I go on?"

"No, that's quite enough, I believe you," I answered. He knew his stuff alright. "The pandemic was kicking off just as I left."

"About this person who sent you here," said Thomas. "Do you know why, exactly?"

"It all happened quite quickly," I replied. "I met him in a pub. He was about fifty in 2020, that's why I wondered if it might have been you. He had overheard me talking about the events of today to the regulars. He followed me into the toilets and offered me the chance to come back and put things right. Obviously, I didn't believe him for a moment."

"Yet here you are," said Thomas. "Are you sure this man offered you the chance to change history? That seems very irresponsible. What exactly did he say?"

"He said I could go back in time for a day, do whatever I wanted, and then go back to 2020."

"And everything would be changed?" asked Thomas.

"He didn't say that exactly," I admitted. "I just assumed that's what he meant. I wasn't taking it seriously because I thought he was just some crackpot."

"But he wasn't because you are here," replied Thomas.

"True, but I didn't know that then. But as soon as I arrived in 1988, it was clear what I needed to do. My life in the future's a mess, and it all stemmed from what would have happened with Charlotte today."

"So, you changed it."

"Of course," I replied. "One tiny change, that's all I needed to make to change everything. Now I've done it and created a better life for myself in the future."

"But you can't guarantee that," he protested. "Messing about with the timeline could lead to far-reaching changes way beyond what you envisaged. You have no idea what sort of future you might be going back to. The consequences could be catastrophic."

"Oh, don't be so melodramatic" I exclaimed. "This only affects me and Charlotte, not the future of the entire space-time continuum!"

"And what about the baby? You said she got pregnant."

"Two babies," I replied. "I was coerced into marrying the stupid cow after the first one, and we ended up with another a couple of years later."

"Even worse," said Thomas. "That's two people who will never be born if you don't get together with Charlotte. Have you thought about the long-term consequences of that? And not just that, they're your children! You must have realised that you'll never see them again. How do you feel about that?"

I shrugged my shoulders. "Sure, I loved being with the kids when they were growing up, but they've long since flown the nest. They rarely have anything to do with me these days. Besides, I'll probably have other kids – with someone better than her, hopefully, if I got to university as planned. Better genes make better kids. They might make more of their lives, become stockbrokers, or bankers and make some decent money rather than wasting their time on teaching and nursing like the two I had before."

Thomas stared at me with a look of utter disbelief on his face. I had shocked him. I liked doing that to people.

"Do you realise what you're saying? he asked. "You've just callously condemned your children to death! And what does it matter what they do for a living? A nurse may not earn as much as a banker, but I know which one I'd have more respect for."

"Look, it's hardly as if I'm murdering them in cold blood, is it? They will never have existed in the other timeline. When I get back to 2020, I might not even remember them, so it won't matter to me, anyway. I'm not exactly sure how this all works."

"But it does matter," protested Thomas. "Everything you do, every interaction both you and Charlotte have will be different. It will send shockwaves outwards, contaminating everything and everyone you touch. By the time you return to 2020, the world might be unrecognisable from the one you left. What if there has been a nuclear war or something? This could backfire on you, spectacularly!"

"Oh, come on," I replied. "Charlotte and I aren't that important in the wider scheme of things. Well, she isn't anyway. I'm anticipating being a lot more important in the new timeline. I'll probably end up as CEO of a big FTSE 100 company, or something like that. But starting a nuclear war? That's ridiculous."

"I'm sorry, but I simply cannot allow you to do this," said Thomas, looking at me with a serious look on his face.

If he was trying to intimidate me, he wasn't succeeding. I wasn't fazed in the slightest.

"Who are you, the time travel police? Exactly how do you plan to stop me?" I asked, smirking.

"I thought when we came in here that I might be able to appeal to your better nature," he said. "However, it's abundantly clear now that you don't have one."

"You're right, I don't," I replied. "And what's more, I couldn't care less. This is all academic, anyway, because the deed is already done. I don't see how you're going to stop me doing something I've already done."

"Not necessarily," he said. "Maybe if you went back to the pub and apologised, you might be able to turn things around."

"I don't think so," I replied. "Even if I wanted to, you heard what I said to her. Who would forgive that? And it's gone half-two anyway, so the pub will be closed, by now."

"Go and find her in college, then. Please, I need you to do this. If not for you, then for me."

"For you? I never do anything for anyone unless there's something in it for me. Why should I possibly want to do anything for you? Especially something that means screwing up my own future."

"You screwed up your future a long time ago," he replied. But I've got a wife and daughter waiting for me in my future and if you interfere with the timeline now, I might never meet them."

"That's your problem, mate," I replied.

"Seriously, I've been going out of my way to keep the timeline on track, not do anything to alter it, and it was all going along swimmingly until you showed up."

"Oh, well I'm so sorry I didn't consult you first, since you seem to have made yourself the self-appointed guardian of the timeline," I said. "Who is this wife, anyway? You know who she is, and when you'll meet her, presumably. What can anything I do possibly interfere with that?"

"Her name's Sarah, and I will meet her ten years from now. By that time, your meddling might have made that impossible."

"Absolute bollocks," I replied. "In the remote likelihood anything I did today does change things then you've got a whole decade to sort it out. Adapt, and work around it. Now, quite honestly, I've had enough of this. I'm keen to get back to 2020 and start my new life."

Then a deliciously evil thought struck me.

"Hey, here's an idea. Since you've got nothing better to do, why don't you go and find Charlotte? She's probably looking for a shoulder to cry on and that's when women are at their most vulnerable, in my experience. I reckon you could probably give her one today if you play your cards right. She was still a decent shag in 1988 before she went all saggy. Your wife won't mind, you don't meet her for another decade."

I drained the last of my coffee, pushed my chair in, and put my coat on, ready to brave the snow outside. Thomas just sat there with a horrified look on his face.

"Nothing to say?" I asked, teasingly.

"You…you're a monster!" was all he could muster.

"Oh, get over yourself," I said, enjoying his discomfort. "You've got an amazing gift. How many people can see the future? Possibly no-one else in the whole world but us two. Forget all this protecting the timeline rubbish and make the most of it - I would. Sadly, I'm off back to the future tomorrow, more's the pity, so I won't get the chance."

"Thank goodness for that," said Thomas. "You've done quite enough damage already."

"Oh, the day's young yet," I said. "Who knows what else I might do. See you later!"

With that parting remark, I turned my back on him and left, striding purposefully out of the café. I wanted to make him sweat a bit. He was probably sitting there now wondering what more evil deeds I might do.

Truth be told, I was devoid of ideas. The coffee hadn't done anything to stimulate me and it had been a good hour or more now since I'd had any alcohol. I was beginning to feel a bit rough. There wasn't a lot else I could do as I only had a couple of quid left. I had a cashpoint card but couldn't remember the PIN.

I wandered around Oxford for a while, feeling nostalgic, but it was simply too cold to stay outside for long. I was starting to feel hungry, so I bought a doughnut for 30p from the fondly remembered Don Miller's Bread Kitchen.

I quickly polished off my deliciously sugary treat, whilst wondering why this place had disappeared. It had been incredibly popular with locals, workers, and students alike for years. It always seemed to be doing a roaring trade, even on a freezing day like this.

Opposite Don Miller's, in Bonn Square, was a homeless man dressed in a stripy, woollen hat and a green trench coat. He had a grey straggly beard and a black Labrador by his side. I remembered this man from my youth, always swigging cheap cider and shouting at the pigeons.

He was one of those men of indeterminate age which could have been anywhere between forty and seventy. He seemed to have been there forever, and I had no idea how either he or the dog survived. I didn't like people like him. I thought they lowered the tone of the city.

As I passed, he held out a white, plastic cup to me and said "10p for a cup of tea, guv?"

I gave him a dirty look. As if I was going to give him any money, and besides, where could you get a cup of tea for 10p, even in 1988? Ordinarily, I wouldn't have said anything, but I felt invincible today.

"You'll only spend it on Diamond White," I said, noting the empty bottle beside him.

"Karma's waiting for you," he muttered in reply as if he was some wise, old sage. What was it with these tramps and winos, coming out with these prophetic statements? If he was that bloody clever, then how did he end up sitting on a blanket in the snow begging for pennies to spend on super-strength cider?

I'd had enough of hanging around Oxford. I had achieved all I could here and all I cared about now was getting back to 2020 to see the results. I caught the bus home, went straight up to my room, and fell asleep, grunting only that I wasn't hungry when my mum woke me up briefly to ask if I wanted any supper.

After that, I slept soundly for a good twelve hours. I had been fully expecting to wake up in a bright new future, a world away from the horrible bedsit I had ended up in. During the night I had dreams about where my new life might take me. I dreamt of a riverside pad in London, close to the Canary Wharf, with a trophy wife, a flash car and all the trappings of the lifestyle that was rightfully mine.

When I awoke, it was to discover that I wasn't in London, but I wasn't in the bedsit either. It was dark, with the only light in the room coming from the red LED alarm clock next to my bed displaying the time at 6:56. It was the very clock that had sat on my bedside table throughout my teenage years.

A quick dash to the window was all it took to confirm it. I opened the curtains and looked out to see that the streetlight behind the house had snowflakes whirling in front of it, like a flurry of moths in the summer. It was casting enough light for me to recognise the familiar scene I had grown up seeing from my window.

I was still in 1988.

Chapter Five - Thomas

My encounter with Ben had been a sobering experience. I had been sailing along simply fine beforehand, fully in control of my abilities, enjoying my life, and confident I had it on track. Now I wasn't so sure.

I had been lulled into a false sense of security with the assumption that only I knew the future. It had been naïve and presumptuous. I wouldn't be so complacent again.

It was Sunday afternoon, two days after the encounter with Ben, and I was lying on my bed listening to the Top 40 on Radio One. This was something I did most weekends, particularly at this time of year when it was dark by teatime.

I was listening to a song entitled *Wild Hearted Woman* by All About Eve which had gone up one place to No. 33. Although this was the first song of theirs that I had become aware of, I felt an instant affinity with the band. It brought with it a premonition of seeing them live at The Royal Albert Hall. This was something that would undoubtedly happen in the future.

I also had an uneasy feeling that something bad was going to happen to this band on Top of the Pops sometime soon, but I couldn't put my finger on it. Doubtless, I would find out in the fullness of time.

I mulled over recent events and their potential implications. Whoever had sent Ben back in time couldn't have chosen a worse person. I had not had any significant interaction with him before Friday, but I had seen enough to peg him as an obnoxious pain in the arse. And that was just his original self. The older version who had taken over the younger body had taken things to a whole new level. He was truly reprehensible.

At least he had only been here for one day. The thought of the monster I had drunk coffee with being given free rein in this time didn't bear thinking about. I wondered if his younger self would be aware of what had gone on when his older mind left the body.

If not, then perhaps all was not lost. Could I manipulate the situation to ensure he and Charlotte still got together? It would be a tall order after his performance on Friday but not impossible.

Even if I couldn't, he had been right about one thing. It was just a small local affair, which might only affect that lives of him, Charlotte, and the other people close to them, at least for the next ten years. That was all the time I needed. Did it matter what happened after that?

Whichever way, I was confident I could handle it. What I wasn't so sure about was whether this was a one-off incident. How many more people could there be messing about in time? And how would I even know about it? I had been lucky this time that the person sent back in time coincidentally happened to be someone in my social circle.

That wouldn't always be the case. But then, if there were other time travellers out there, changing things, wouldn't

I have noticed by now? Everything seemed as it should, and my visions were as reliable as ever. Maybe this was just a one-off incident. Nevertheless, I vowed to be more vigilant from now on. I would keep my eyes open locally, analyse every news report, and read the newspaper from cover to cover each day.

It was nearly 7pm now and I switched off the radio in disgust as I heard that Bros had climbed to No. 2 in the chart. I hoped they didn't make it to the top. I honestly couldn't remember if they did or not, my memory didn't recall every fact and figure. I couldn't stand Bros and what was worse, half the blokes in college seemed to be copying their haircuts, including, of course, Ben.

It was good timing as my mother was calling me from downstairs for our traditional Sunday roast. This turned out to be chicken with all the trimmings, including pigs in blankets. A lot of people only had them at Christmas, but we always had them with chicken, which we had every four weeks on a cycle that went beef – pork – lamb – chicken – repeat.

The weather was much improved the following day, with the sun putting in a rare appearance, melting the remaining snow. Not only was it the first day of a new week, but it was also the first of a new month. What would February bring? For the first time in this life, I couldn't be certain that the days would pan out exactly the way I pictured them.

I had decided what to do about Ben and Charlotte, and I quickened my pace as I took the short walk to the bus stop. I was keen to get started. The low, winter sun was incredibly bright, giving the illusion of warmth, but the air was freezing, and I could see condensation forming in front of me with each breath.

I was warmed by the sight of a large cluster of snowdrops that had flowered on the grass verge behind the bus stop. There was something I loved about these flowers. They signalled rebirth, of life beginning anew in the first flush of spring. It was something I identified with as I was like those snowdrops, born anew with fresh hope.

After my first lecture, I headed over to the pub. It was much quieter than it had been on Friday, but Charlotte and her friends were seated at their usual table by the jukebox. I had never really spoken to her before and wasn't sure how to begin the conversation. Then I saw she was wearing an All About Eve t-shirt. That would give me something to break the ice with.

I sauntered casually over to the three of them, who were sitting quietly, smoking away. Charlotte's pallor seemed even more deathly white than usual. She had gone to town on the makeup this morning. As I approached, she looked up and blew a perfect smoke ring in my direction. This unnerved me, causing me to stumble over my words.

"Er, hi, it's Charlotte, isn't it?" I mumbled.

This was pathetic. I sounded like some nervous fifteen-year-old trying to ask a girl out on a date.

"Who wants to know?" she replied, aloofly.

"I couldn't help noticing you were wearing an All About Eve t-shirt," I began. "I heard them on the radio yesterday. They're awesome!"

"You're right, they are," she said, looking me up and down, taking in my white t-shirt and jeans. "I saw them at Reading last year. You know, I must say, you don't strike me as an obvious fan."

"Just because I don't dress all in black and cover myself with crucifixes doesn't mean I don't appreciate good music," I replied, hoping this wouldn't offend. But my mind was quickly put at rest. She was beginning to engage with me.

"I've got a tape with their latest single and the B-sides in my bag," she said. "Why don't you meet me in the library later, and we can listen to it on my Walkman?"

As she said this, she winked at me. This was promising; it showed that she liked me. Not too much, I hoped. I didn't want this to go any further than necessary. I was already breaking my non-interference rules just by approaching her.

"Actually, there was something else I wanted to talk to you about," I said.

"It can wait until later," she said. "I'll be in the library at three. Or we could meet in the student union office if you like? I've got a key. It'll be more private."

"The library will be just fine," I replied, hastily, remembering what Ben had said about what she liked to do in that office.

"Good," she said, turning away from me and back to her friends, making it clear the conversation was over for the time being.

I went and ordered a drink from Arthur and then joined a few of the other lads for a game of darts. Of Ben, there was no sign, thank goodness. I needed to speak to Charlotte before I tackled him.

True to her word, she was waiting for me in the library, wisely choosing a table as far away as possible from the imposing figure of Joan the librarian. She could detect a pin drop at fifty feet and had the loudest shush in the world.

"Check this out," said Charlotte, as I sat down, passing me a set of fuzzy orange headphones.

"Oh, cool," I said, catching sight of her Walkman. "You've got one of those new ones with two headphone sockets."

"Better with two," she said, winking again. "Come on, don't be shy."

The wires on the headphones weren't long, meaning there was no way for us both to listen without getting up close and personal. She pulled another chair alongside hers and patted it, beckoning me to sit down. It was all rather more intimate than I felt comfortable with, and although the music was great, her proximity wasn't.

I could hear her breathing and see the light rise and fall of her breasts as she did so. I felt a flush of attraction and I sensed that she felt the same. The air was almost crackling with the sexual tension. This wasn't what I'd come here for, and when she turned to try and kiss me, it took all my willpower to tear myself away. This wouldn't do at all!

"Whoa, what are you doing?" I exclaimed, taking the headphones off, and pushing the chair back. Unfortunately, I didn't get them off in time to judge the volume of my voice, earning a stern shush from Joan at the other end of the room.

"I'm sorry," she said, "I thought you liked me. Pretending to be into All About Eve even though you dress more like a Wet Wet Wet fan!"

"You thought Ben liked you on Friday and look how that turned out!" I replied.

"Don't talk to me about that arsehole," she said.

But that was exactly what I had come here to do. Persuade her to give him a second chance.

"You know, he's not as bad as he seems," I said, even though I knew that he was every bit as bad as he seemed. Worse, probably.

I felt wretched doing this. Was it fair to Charlotte to try and push her into a life of misery with Ben? I was beginning to question my motives. Ruin her life to protect mine? But it was what should have happened, it was Ben who had changed it, not me. I was just correcting the damage.

"You must be crazy! He's horrible! You were there, you saw what he said to me. I can't believe I ever thought I fancied him. You're much nicer."

"I'm spoken for," I replied.

"I've never seen you with a girl," she said. "Molly thought you might be gay, but I don't think you are. You're not, are you?"

"No, I'm not gay. There is someone, but it's complicated. It's a long-distance relationship sort of thing."

I hoped she would buy this. In a way it was true. Sarah was in Swansea and I was in Oxford, and the long-distance related to time as well as space.

"Oh, that's a pity," she said. "We could have had a lot of fun together."

"I still think Ben's the right one for you," I suggested, without a great deal of conviction. "I think you just caught him on a bad day. Maybe if he were to apologise…?"

"It would have to be one hell of an apology," she exclaimed. "What he did on Friday was unforgivable. What sort of person would people think I was if I still went out with him after all that?"

"But you would consider it?" I asked. "You do still fancy him?"

"Physically, yes, but his personality stinks. I really don't know."

"I know for a fact he likes you," I lied. "Leave it with me, I'll talk to him. Trust me."

"Quite the little matchmaker, aren't you?" said Charlotte. "Go on, then, talk to him, but he's going to have to come up with a spectacular gesture to get anywhere with me now."

And that was as far as the conversation went because, unseen by us, the terrifying presence of Joan, complete with her theatrical Dame Edna style specs, had crept up on us. She ran a tight ship, like an old-fashioned matron on a ward and had grown irritated by our continued conversation. It was made clear I had overstayed my welcome.

No matter, I had achieved part one of the plan. Now all I had to do was find Ben and hope his younger self had no memory of the events of the previous week.

He proved to be an elusive fellow to track down. I scoured the college but to no avail. It was the same story the next day, but I did speak to his friend, Mark, who was on the same course. He was in the refectory, on his own, eating a dubious-looking sausage roll.

"Have you seen anything of Ben?" I asked.

"Haven't seen him since Friday," replied Mark, munching away. "And I'm quite glad about it. I reckon he's probably lying low for a while."

"Do you know where he lives?" I asked.

"Somewhere up Cumnor Hill I think," he replied. "He never let us go to his house. He said something about us lowering the tone of the neighbourhood."

That sounded like Ben. It wasn't particularly helpful, but then just turning up at his house unannounced probably wouldn't be a good idea even if I did have his address.

"Is there anywhere else I might find him?"

"I know he goes to Parkers on Wednesday nights and meets up with a couple of guys from his rugby team. He says he does, anyway. We were never allowed to go there with him because he said we didn't fit the demographic. I'm not even sure what that means."

I knew what it meant, and it was exactly the sort of thing Ben was likely to say. I'd never been to Parkers and wasn't sure I'd be able to get in. I hadn't turned eighteen yet, so getting served could be an issue. It was the only lead I had, though, so I'd have to give it a shot.

Parkers was an upmarket venue on St Clements, and I felt a little intimidated on my approach the following evening. I could see through the large, glass frontage the well-heeled groups of young people clinking cocktail glasses. It was a world away from The Duke. There wouldn't be any pints of mild being served up in this place.

I spotted Ben right away, not wearing one of his usual cashmere jumpers, but a red and black rugby shirt. He was standing at the bar with two similarly dressed lads. As I approached all three of them banged three times on the bar, lifted shots of what looked like rum, and shouted out "down the hatch!"

They then proceeded to knock the shots back in one before making a full 360-degree turn and grabbing three pints of lager from the bar which they also attempted to down in one, with varying degrees of success. At least half of Ben's appeared to go down his shirt.

"Three more pints and three more shots, my good fellow," said one of Ben's friends, in a cut-glass accent that reeked of money and privilege. As he did so, Ben caught sight of me.

"Well, well, if it isn't my favourite little feminist, Thomas. Chaps, this is the fellow I was telling you about."

The two of them turned to look down their noses at me, drunkenly swaying on their feet as they did so.

"These are my friends, Jonty and Julian," said Ben. "Jonty's father is a barrister and Julian is the son of a stockbroker. We all play on the same rugby team."

Jonty looked me up and down, with no attempt to conceal his disdain.

"A little underdressed for this place, aren't you, old boy? I didn't realise they were letting people in jeans in here these days. You really ought to mix with a better class of person, Ben."

"Excuse me one moment, chaps," said Ben, grabbing my arm and steering me away from the bar. As soon as we were out of earshot, he turned on me, clearly not at all pleased at me having the audacity to speak to him in front of his posh friends.

"What the fuck are you doing here?" he asked, coarsely. "People like us come here to get away from people like you."

This was a more aggressive response than I was expecting, and it made me uneasy. I knew that the younger version of Ben was unpleasant, but I hadn't expected him to be as hostile as his older counterpart.

"I came to give you a message," I began. "It's from Charlotte."

"Didn't I tell you last Friday, I wanted nothing to do with that slag?" he said.

"You remember, then?" I asked.

My whole strategy was based around him not remembering. This didn't bode well.

"Of course, I remember," he said. "I was there, wasn't I? You're the one that seems to be suffering from amnesia."

"But you shouldn't remember," I protested. "You said that whoever sent you was going to take you back to your own time after twenty-four hours! You should be the younger version of you again."

"Well, I guess whoever he was, he must have forgotten," said Ben, looking pleased with himself. "I'm still here. And you know what? I'm loving it. I've had five days to think about all the things I can do, and the possibilities are endless. I've been given a superpower and I'm going to use it to get everything I've ever wanted. And there's absolutely nothing you can do to stop me!"

I didn't like the sound of that at all.

Chapter Six - Ben

1988. A time of opportunity.

I didn't know why I hadn't returned to 2020, and I didn't care. The stranger who sent me here had broken his promise to return me after twenty-four hours and I was thrilled about it.

I thought I would be here for one day, just long enough to make a change that would give me a shot at a better future. But not having to return at all well and truly trumped that. It was the best thing that could have happened.

What fifty-year-old would refuse the chance to hit the reset button and go back to the age of eighteen? No matter how successful they had been, or how happy they were, surely, they wouldn't turn the offer down?

It was an extra thirty-two years of life for a start which would come with a bonus of three decades of hindsight and experience. How many times had I heard people say, "if I'd only known what I know now when I was young?" Well, I did know and the potential power at my fingertips was awe-inspiring.

I knew about future world events. I knew the outcome of major sporting championships. I could bet on them and make a fortune or change things if I wanted to. As a Liverpool supporter, I'd had thirty years of people ribbing me about them failing to win the league. Just as it looked like they were finally going to do it in 2020, I'd been denied the chance to celebrate by being sent back here.

How about I got rich, bought the club and sunk billions into them? That would wipe the grin off the faces of those smug, self-satisfied Man United supporters.

It wouldn't matter that this would rip up the form book and alter all the future results because I'd already have made my billions by then. I wouldn't need to bet anymore.

Why stop there? I could shape the whole future of the world if I so desired. The new 2020 could look vastly different from the one I'd left. I could be Prime Minister and Boris Johnson might still be editing The Spectator for a living.

As for Thomas and his wittering on about protecting the timeline, well screw him! I could do whatever the hell I wanted. I don't know why he wasn't doing it already. I would have been, in his position, rather than going all slushy over some bird he hadn't even met yet.

Where to start? I already had, by taking down Charlotte. I was proud of my performance in the pub on Friday. I had been fearless and ruthless – qualities that all those who aspire to true greatness need to possess.

Now that I was stuck in 1988, I needed to get a bit wiser about how I dealt with people. I hadn't cared on Friday when I thought I was only around for the day, but now I needed to keep certain people on my side. It was only for a while until I had used them to get where I wanted to go. If I said the right things and greased the right palms, I could rapidly make my way to the top. By the time people realised I was a wolf in sheep's clothing, it would be too late.

The first thing I needed to do was make myself rich. Money talked and I couldn't walk the walk and talk the talk without looking the part. Posh jumpers had served me well to this point, but once I had wealth, I'd be heading for Savile Row.

I could start this very year by finding as much money as possible to lump on Rhyme and Reason in The Grand National. Once I had done that, I'd just build up my pot. One horse I was particularly waiting for was Norton's Coin, the 100/1 winner of the 1990 Cheltenham Gold Cup. I remember my grandfather had 50p each way on that. Pathetic! I'd have thousands to put on it by then.

Then I could invest in other areas. Imagine getting in on Amazon and Google at the beginning! I'd be looking down on The Queen and Richard Branson from the top of The Sunday Times Rich List by the turn of the century.

It wasn't just money I was after. I wanted respect, power, and people to look up to me. All the things I had found elusive in my previous life. I wanted people to adore me and see me as a national hero.

I immediately ditched my plans to go to college to get a degree. Having a lucrative career in stockbroking or banking simply didn't cut it anymore. That was for mere mortals. And I simply didn't have time to waste years on a degree. I wanted it all and I wanted it quickly. I wanted to become one of the most powerful people, like Donald Trump. I had always admired him and couldn't understand why people didn't like him.

Well, with the advantages I had I could eclipse him. Sure, I liked the guy and I'd invite him over to play on one of my golf courses in the future, providing he knew that I was more important than him. I could be bigger than anyone. I could even give God a run for his money if he existed.

The possibilities were endless, and I spent most of Saturday and Sunday holed up in my room plotting and planning. The winter weather hadn't abated so there wasn't much else I could do anyway.

My parents didn't take a lot of notice of me over the weekend, but then they never had. My recollections of my teenage years were that they were totally out of touch with modern culture. They had no interest whatsoever in things like pop music and completely misjudged the potential of computers, dismissing them as a fad. Back here in 1988, they were behaving exactly as I had remembered.

None of my friends attempted to contact me over the weekend. That was no surprise after Friday when they had said they didn't want to hang out with me anymore. It didn't bother me in the slightest. I did not need people like Mark and Adam. I had only ever kept them around because I liked to feel superior to working-class trash like them.

I had my sights set now on mixing with a far better class of person. There were a couple of guys who went to one of Oxford's private schools I was keen to look up again. We were part of the same local rugby club and I had done my best to ingratiate myself with them, but it was always a little difficult.

They were stinking rich and looked down at me the same way I looked down at Adam and Mark. This class system was endemic in British culture where there was an unspoken pecking order. It was time for me to move up that food chain.

I had done my best to fit in with them the first time around by talking knowledgeably about the stock market, flashing my Filofax and poking fun at Sun readers. It worked to a degree but there was always this aura they gave off around me that hinted they knew I wasn't one of them and never would be.

Despite being relatively well off compared to the other kids at my local primary school, I had failed the entrance exams to get into two of Oxford's most prestigious private schools. This left only one unpalatable alternative left – a local comprehensive.

My father wasn't pleased. He had harboured high hopes for me and seemed to lose interest in me after I failed to get in. I'm convinced the entrance exam was fixed because let's face it, there's no way all those other kids could have been cleverer than me, even if they had gone to The Dragon School. I think they deliberately discriminated against me.

The school I eventually ended up at was every bit as ghastly as I had feared. It was a grey, soulless institution which

I left under a cloud of underachievement. I was convinced that I was being victimised by certain teachers who didn't like me for some reason.

With my poor set of O Level grades, I ended up with the other plebs at the local tech which wasn't something that was going to impress the likes of Jonty and Julian. I avoided mentioning this and did my utmost to keep my other friends away from them, but invariably, my acquaintance with them fizzled out.

In my first life, the only thing we had in common was rugby, and when they moved on to University, they joined their college teams. I was left behind, stuck with Charlotte and the baby.

That wasn't going to happen again. I was determined to gain their respect, and not just theirs – other people's too. I didn't care that Thomas didn't agree with what I was doing or that he thought I was a bad person. That was his problem. I didn't need to impress him.

It would be a lot easier to get to where I wanted to be in 1988 than it would have been in 2020. I didn't have to worry about constantly saying or doing the right things to avoid getting cancelled. This was the fate of many who wouldn't play ball in the ultra-woke culture of 2020. Here, where social media hadn't been invented yet, I had the freedom to do and say whatever I wanted. I didn't have to worry that my every move might be filmed, photographed, and splashed all over the internet.

1988 was refreshingly free of such crap. If you weren't there and didn't see it, then there was no record. There would be no incriminating tweets or ill-considered Facebook comments to be dredged up and used against me in the future. I couldn't go wrong.

It was a couple of months until the Grand National so I thought I might lay some groundwork for the future by nurturing my friendships with my affluent friends. A quick scan through my Filofax revealed Jonty's phone number, so on Monday evening, I gave him a ring.

One of the bugbears of using old-fashioned landlines in this era was you couldn't guarantee you'd get the person you wanted to speak to on the other end. That was the case on this occasion when Jonty's father answered.

"Oh, good evening, Mr Barrington-Smythe," I began, trying to sound as posh as possible. "May I speak with Jonty, please?"

"Jonathon!" bellowed his father. "Someone on the telephone for you!"

"Who is it?" came the distant reply from afar. I hadn't realised Jonty was short for Jonathon. I had never heard anyone use his full name before.

"To whom do I have the pleasure of speaking?" asked Jonty's father rather formally.

"It's Ben Lewis," I replied. "I'm a friend of Jonty's from the rugby club."

I wished I had a more impressive surname. Perhaps that's something else I could change. Double-barrelled surnames were good.

"It's Ben," said his father.

"Ben who?" asked Jonty. "I don't know anyone called Ben."

That was Jonty, all over. What a card, pretending he didn't know me.

"Lewis, I think he said," replied his father.

There was a pause, then I heard him say, "Oh – him. What does he want?"

"Perhaps you ought to speak with him," said his father, and there was a thud as he put the handset down on a hard surface. After more crackling, Jonty's dulcet tones came through.

"Lewis, you oik, what do you mean by phoning me at home at this time? We're about to have our supper."

There followed a little light-hearted banter before I managed to wheedle out of him that he and Julian were going for Wednesday night cocktails after rugby practice. When I suggested I join them, he didn't sound thrilled but reluctantly agreed.

"Go on then, I suppose you can tag along, but make sure you wear some decent clothes. Daddy says it's important to be seen with the right people. He'd have a fit if he knew you'd been to a comprehensive."

Speak of the devil, I heard his father's voice, booming out in the background.

"What's that, Daddy? Oh, right, I must go, Benson is serving the starters. See you on Wednesday, town boy."

And with that, he hung up.

I wasn't too happy about him calling me town boy. A phrase often bandied around Oxford was town and gown, distinguishing the town's indigenous working population from the academic elite. It was one of Jonty's little ways of letting me know which he considered I belonged to.

It hadn't bothered me so much in the past, but Jonty's condescending manner irked me far more in my new circumstances. In a few short years, the likes of him would be bowing and scraping to me. In the meantime, I would absorb the insults until I had used him and his ilk to help get me to where I wanted to be.

Wednesday night rugby went well. I was amazed at how light and agile my body felt without years of wear and tear to hinder it. Even the wet and cold weather on the rugby field didn't bother me. I felt young, strong, and invincible.

I carried that confidence forward into Parkers where we began with expensive cocktails before embarking on various drinking challenges. I was spending rather more than I could afford at this time. I hadn't had time to use my knowledge to make any money yet and it was vital I kept up the appearance of wealth until then.

All was going swimmingly until that idiot Thomas turned up, embarrassing me in front of my friends. I took him to one side at which point he made some ridiculous suggestion about getting back with Charlotte.

I took great delight in disappointing him. First, I told him that I had no intention of having anything to do with Charlotte. Then I dropped the bombshell that he was still dealing with the future version of me. He was horrified, much to my amusement.

He then started banging on about corrupting the timeline again. I cut him short and agreed to meet him the following day at lunchtime if he went away and stopped cramping my style in front of my influential friends.

I didn't know why I agreed to meet him again. It was clear what his agenda was – to stop me from doing the things I wanted to do but I didn't see how he could, short of killing me. And I doubted he would have the guts for that. But I needed to ascertain how big a thorn in my side he was going to be, and I could only do that by talking to him.

It was very much a case of keeping your friends close and your enemies closer. Find out what his intentions were and then combat them accordingly. What was the best way to play it? I could keep my cards close to my chest, promise to be a good boy, and not interfere with the timeline. Then, hopefully, he would go away.

But that wasn't in my nature. Why should I have to justify myself to him? It would be far more fun to tell him all the things I was going to do and watch his reaction. If he wanted to go to war with me, then bring it on. If things escalated, I was confident I could be far more ruthless than him.

We met the following lunchtime at The Marlborough Arms, another lost pub from the past. It backed directly on to Morrells Brewery which was very convenient as they didn't have to wait for deliveries. They just rolled the barrels in through the back gate.

The lunchtime clientele consisted largely of the brewery workers, sampling the very product they spent all week producing. It wasn't the sort of place I'd be seen dead in normally, but then that wasn't something I needed to worry about. The calibre of people in the sort of circles I intended to mix would be unlikely to stray into this cultural backwater.

Thomas asked me what my plans were, so I began by talking about how I intended to acquire my wealth.

"Betting on the horses?" he replied. "Bit old hat, isn't it? I've been doing it on the Grand National for years."

"Then you're a hypocrite," I replied. "You give me a ton of grief about changing the timeline and here you are admitting to doing it yourself."

"In a small way," he replied. "Not enough to make any material difference. You're talking about making millions. That changes things."

"How?" I enquired, keen to hear his theory. If there were any pitfalls to what I had planned, it would be useful to find out before I started.

"In the same way that a huge meteorite hitting the sea is different from you or me chucking a pebble in. The effect spreads outwards. You'll alter the price of the horse for a start which affects everyone who bets on the race."

"But it will still win, so who cares," I boasted. "If I take the price before the race, it's not going to affect me, is it? They'll have to pay me out at the price they agreed."

"You're assuming you can get the bet on," he said. "What do you think the bookies will do if you start winning all the time. Keep letting you fleece them, or ban you from the betting shop? It does happen, you know."

"Oh, I'll find a way," I boasted, confidently. "Why don't you do the same? Is it really worth pinning all your hopes on meeting this Sarah in ten years when you could have everything you've ever wanted? I'm going to be rich, driving fast cars, and partying with supermodels. Can you seriously tell me you don't want a piece of that?"

"It's about things you'll never understand, Ben," he replied. "Things like loyalty and love, concepts that seem to be completely beyond you, by my observations. Though, to be fair, you clearly love yourself."

"I do," I said. "And the rest of the world will love me soon too. Because I'm going to be a hero."

"You, a hero?" he asked. "I find that most unlikely. How exactly?"

"By righting wrongs and saving lives," I replied. "Yeah, you didn't expect that, did you? Maybe I'm not the uncaring swine you take me for."

"Forgive me if I sound sceptical but you're hardly the sort of person to go around doing good deeds for the fun of it."

"You're right, I'm not!" I replied. "It will all be to further my interests. But no-one will know that when the country's hailing me a hero."

"OK, so what are you planning to do?" he asked.

"Disaster prevention," I replied. "There were loads of them during this era. Hardly a year went by without some major catastrophe or other. Fires, planes crashing, ferries sinking. All preventable, for the most part, if you know in advance."

"Really," he said. "How exactly do you intend to prevent these disasters? It might not be as easy as you think."

"Easy. Let's take that fire at King's Cross last year. If I had been around then I could have set the fire alarms off before the fire broke out. Everyone evacuated, and everyone safe."

"And how exactly does that make you a hero?" he asked. "From what I recall that fire was started by someone dropping a lit cigarette. It fell through an old wooden staircase on to a pile of litter below. It was an accident waiting to happen. If you cause an evacuation before that cigarette gets dropped, the fire won't start."

"Exactly, think of all those lives saved," I said.

"But how will anyone know?" asked Thomas. "If there's no fire, no-one will know you saved any lives. What are you going to do? Stand outside the station and tell everyone who comes out how you've saved their lives? You're more likely to get arrested for setting the fire alarm off."

Thomas was irritating me. He had spotted a flaw in my plan that I hadn't considered and was now looking back at me with a smug look on his face. He thought he was cleverer than me, but he wasn't. He just had more experience with this sort of thing.

"All right, clever dick," I said. "I haven't finalised all the details yet, it's still a work in progress."

This didn't deter him, and he continued to pick holes in my idea.

"It's probably also worth pointing out that you might not save any lives in the long run. If the fire doesn't happen, the appropriate lessons won't be learned, and it will happen at some point, a few weeks, or months down the road anyway. All you'll be doing is delaying the inevitable. But it will be different people who die – and I don't need to begin to tell you the implications of that."

"Yeah, I know," I replied. "Your precious, beloved timeline. OK, how about this then? What if I had waited until the fire had already started before raising the alarm. The blaze would still have happened, but I would have rescued everyone."

"Well, I guess we'll never know because it's already happened, so unless you have some way of going further back in time, you may as well forget it."

"I was only using King's Cross as an example," I said. "There are plenty of other disasters yet to happen. Lockerbie, 9/11, you name it."

"You're playing with fire," said Thomas. "You have no idea what the implications of interfering with those events could be. They are part of a global terror network for a start. Do you really want to bring yourself to the attention of those people? They might not look too kindly on someone foiling their carefully planned atrocities."

"Fair point," I replied, in a rare concession to someone else's point of view. Thomas may have been a pain in the arse, but he did know his stuff, and he hadn't finished yet.

"Also, how do you think the world's intelligence services will react to someone popping up with foreknowledge of terrorist attacks? Do you think they're going to pat you on the back and congratulate you on a job well done?"

"They might," I replied, unconvincingly.

"I think it's more likely that they might question how you came to possess this knowledge. And you know what happens to people who know too much. They have a nasty habit of disappearing."

"OK, you've made your point. I'll avoid anything terrorism-related and stick to accidents and natural disasters."

"You should avoid all of it," said Thomas. "It's not just about me and Sarah, you're messing with people's lives. And I don't see what the big attraction is of doing this anyway. Can't you just stick to your other plan of betting on the horses? You can make yourself rich and have a nice life without massively changing things."

"The attraction is that I know I can do it," I replied. People have been going to churches and praying to God for centuries without knowing whether he exists or not. Well now he does, and he is me."

"Are you serious?" he asked, looking at me incredulously. You think you're God?"

"Absolutely," he said. "I've got power, and I'm going to use it. Benevolently, of course. Well, unless people piss me off, of course."

"Then, what?" he asked. "A plague of locusts?"

"Ha, you're funny, aren't you?" I replied. "Take it easy. Just because I've got the power of life and death over everyone in the world doesn't mean I have to use it."

"That's what all power-crazed madmen say," said Thomas. "How long before you're holed up in some bunker-like some megalomaniac James Bond villain."

"Oh, it needn't come to that," I said dismissively. "That all sounds like a lot of hard work. I just want to know I can do it, that's all. And then there's the fact that you don't approve. I don't like people telling me what to do and not to do. That's like a red rag to a bull to me and makes me want to do it just to piss you off."

"I'll stop you," he said, but he wasn't convincing. I could hear the weakness in his voice. He had temporarily gained the upper hand in the conversation a few moments ago, but now I was firmly back on top.

"I'd like to see you try," I replied. "I've already got something lined up for next month."

"What is it?" he asked. "Tell me!"

Should I tell him? If I did, might he try and stop me? Then again, that was all part of the fun. If I didn't tell him, he wouldn't know about it and wouldn't be around when it happened. Sod it, I would tell him. I wanted him to see the look of triumph on my face when I successfully screwed with history.

"Fair enough if you insist. Do you remember the Devon rail disaster?"

"No," said Thomas. "Should I?"

"Good, well you won't mind me preventing it then," I declared.

"Not if I have anything to do with it," he replied.

"You know, I'm so sick of this," I replied. "You come across as all self-righteous and holier than thou. But I'm the one planning to save ninety-eight lives. That's almost a hundred people who never went home to their families that night. But you'd rather let them die. And you think I'm the monster!"

"If they died in that accident, then they were meant to die. From your perspective, it's already happened."

"I disagree. That future has yet to be written. You say I'm wrong to save their lives," I said. "So, by that same logic, standing by and letting them die when I could have saved them is right? You're the monster, mate."

To that, he had no reply at all.

Chapter Seven - Thomas

I didn't see Ben for several weeks after that night at Parkers. What was the point in pursuing him further? Clearly, he wasn't going to take the slightest bit of notice of anything I had to say.

Did it matter that much? I was beginning to think that maybe I had been a little too precious over all of this. It was time to question if my determination to keep the timeline on track had become a little too obsessive. Sarah would almost certainly still be alive and well in 1998, whatever Ben did. Perhaps I should stop stressing over it.

It wasn't as if I hadn't bent the rules from time to time when it suited me, such as avoiding that beating from Gary Roper.

On other occasions, such as having sex with Simone, I had stuck rigidly to the rules. Why had I done that? Was my motivation simply to protect the timeline? Or because it was easy, and enjoyable to have sex with her, even though I had a wife waiting in the future?

I had also admonished Ben for his plans to get rich by using his knowledge to make money from gambling. That was hypocritical, especially as I knew I was going to find it difficult to resist doing the same.

In my past lives, I had done a lot of crappy jobs in my late teens. These included washing-up in restaurants, delivering free property papers, and making sandwiches in the cafeteria at the John Radcliffe Hospital.

Why not avoid all that toil and make my path through life a little smoother? Ben's presence here had changed things. The timeline wouldn't stay on track now, no matter how rigidly I stuck to it. He would see to that.

I had no desire to massively change my life the way I imagine he planned to change his. I would live in the same places and follow the same career path but have a little more fun along the way.

Yes, this would create local ripples, but would any of it spread out enough to affect what was going on in Swansea?

I remained uneasy about what Ben planned to do. My changes would be minor, but he had talked about altering things on a grand scale. That concerned me greatly. He was in the realms of playing with people's lives, deciding who should live or die on a whim. He had even compared himself to God.

Maybe it had just been alcohol-induced boasting that night in Parkers, but if it wasn't, what ought I to do? He had already demonstrated that he wasn't the sort of person who could be reasoned with. All my interventions so far had failed and only seemed to encourage him. He positively enjoyed winding me up.

Perhaps it would be better if I kept my distance from him for a while and let him get on with it. But then, that could be the absolute worst thing to do. I was torn and it wasn't as if there was anyone I could turn to for advice. There hadn't been anyone my whole life.

I decided to bide my time and see what happened. A few weeks passed and I carried on going to college as the weather got better and spring arrived. Of Ben, there was no sign.

I got on with things, enjoyed the rest of the term hanging out with friends, and tried to forget all about him. Then my visions returned.

When he had mentioned a rail disaster to me, I had no recollection of it at the time. He could have been making it up for all I knew. But as Easter approached, disturbing premonitions of the approaching catastrophe began to pop into my mind.

I could see it as clearly as if I were watching it unfold on TV. The Devon rail crash was real and what's more, it was imminent. It reignited my concerns about Ben and what he might be planning. More importantly, whether I ought to do anything about it.

Again, I agonised in solitude about what to do. Then, thanks to a chance encounter in a record store, I wasn't on my own anymore. Suddenly, I had found myself an unexpected ally.

It was the Monday afternoon before Easter and three days before I believed the train crash would take place. I was in HMV looking to buy the new Primitives album, on the strength of their catchy hit, *Crash*, which had recently been riding high in the charts.

I had heard many complaints from friends in the past who had rushed out to buy albums based on the success of one single only to be sorely disappointed.

More savvy music fans preferred to read the reviews in NME and Melody Maker before committing themselves. I didn't have to worry about that. I already knew I loved this album, appropriately titled *Lovely* because in my head I had heard it before.

HMV was my preferred choice of record shop in Oxford. There was also a Virgin Megastore and an Our Price, but there was something special about HMV. I don't know if it was the way it was laid out, the music they played, or the fact that all the cool students hung out there, but I just loved it.

The store had been reorganised recently to give precedence to the fast-emerging compact disc format. Vinyl was less profitable and had been moved to the first floor.

We didn't have a CD player in our house yet, so I headed upstairs. This didn't bother me because I preferred vinyl anyway. Somehow it seemed more real and I loved the lavish, gatefold sleeves you got with many LP's. There was real pride in the artwork which just didn't seem the same shrunk down to a five-inch-tall jewel case.

When I reached the top of the stairs, I spotted an animated looking Charlotte, excitedly clutching a new single to her chest.

She looked up, saw me, and enthusiastically squealed "It's the new All About Eve single! It's out today! Remember when we listened to them in the library?"

She held the single out towards me to show me the cover, revealing her cleavage in the process. Her ever-present crucifix was positioned perfectly between her breasts.

"I do," I replied, forcing my gaze away from her chest and towards the record which had a weird, arty pastiche of a naked man and woman on the cover. There seemed to be breasts everywhere I looked today.

"I also remember you trying to kiss me," I added.

"Yeah, sorry about that," she said, chuckling, before adding unashamedly "I was feeling exceptionally horny that day. What's that you've got there?"

"It's the new album by The Primitives," I replied, turning it around to show her the bold red lettering on the cover.

"Oh, I love them! I really want to hear that. Listen, do you fancy coming back to mine? We could play our new records and have a couple of drinks?"

"I'm not sure," I began, and I meant it. I hadn't forgotten her attempt to pounce on me in the library.

"Don't worry, I won't jump on you again," she said, reading my mind. "We'll just hang out, play some tunes and have a chat. I've got a bottle of Bacardi I've been saving. Fancy it?"

"Why not?" I replied. I may as well. I didn't have anything better to do and it might be fun to spend time with someone with similar music tastes. I knew this was deviating from both our timelines, but hers was already on a different trajectory after Ben's rejection. As for me, well I knew what I was doing. I hoped I did, anyway.

I was surprised when her place turned out not to be her parent's home, as I had expected, but a tiny room in a shared student house on the Cowley Road.

"You're very young to be living on your own," I ventured as we climbed up endless flights of rickety, old stairs. Including the attic, where she resided, the house was a good four storeys high.

"It's a long story," she said. "Let's just say that my stepfather and I don't get along."

The stairs creaked below our feet and I almost slipped on the threadbare carpet. It wasn't the most pleasant of environments. It stank of stale cigarette smoke and I suspected that the yellowish colour of the walls had originally been white.

Underneath a large red switch on the second landing someone had scrawled on the wall in black marker pen the following: *Do not touch this switch. It fucks up the electrics!* There were damp patches on the walls on this floor, one small, filthy window, and cobwebs everywhere.

"Charming place," I said, with more than a hint of sarcasm."

"It's all I could afford," she said. "Twenty-five quid a week."

"How do you pay for it?"

"I work five shifts a week at the 7-11 on the corner. It's enough to scrape by."

We had reached her room, a drab and depressing place, with worn wooden floorboards that had holes the size of golf balls in them. There was also an arch-shaped hole in the skirting board that looked like something out of an old *Tom and Jerry* cartoon. A lick of paint wouldn't have gone amiss.

Other than a double bed and a small table with a portable TV on it, the room was devoid of furniture. Everything else was kept on the floor, including her record player.

"Welcome to my humble abode," she said. "With humble being the operative word. It's not much – but it's mine."

I couldn't help but feel a little sorry for Charlotte. This couldn't be an easy life for an eighteen-year-old. Maybe that was part of the reason for all the dark clothes and gothic paraphernalia. Was it her lonely life in her tiny room that led her to such melancholy? The posters of various Smiths albums and other indie band covers on the wall weren't exactly cheery.

"You have some cool posters," I ventured.

"They cover up the damp patches on the wall," she explained.

"I can well believe it," I said. "Can't you complain to your landlord?"

"You get what you pay for," she replied. "Come on, let's put your album on."

I handed her my purchase, and she drew it carefully and lovingly from the sleeve. A few seconds later, the voice of Tracy Tracy, the oddly named lead singer, began belting out of the speakers.

She produced the promised bottle of Bacardi and a half-drunk bottle of Coke from a cardboard box next to her bed. She poured my drink into an Oxford United mug, and her own into a blue, plastic beaker. These appeared to be the only two cups in the room. Then we sat on the floor next to the record player, as she didn't have any chairs.

"I didn't know you were a football fan," I said as I sipped my drink. The cola was warm and flat, but the rum was warm and powerful, so I didn't mind.

"I'm not," she said. "It was my Dad's. It's one of the few things of his I've got left."

Over the next twenty minutes, I learned about her father's tragically early death from an undiagnosed heart condition. It had happened suddenly, with no warning, when he was in his early forties.

Afterwards, her mother had married a horrible, smarmy man who had sneaked into the bathroom and tried to touch Charlotte up in the shower when she was only sixteen.

When Charlotte confronted her mother over this, she didn't believe her and took her stepfather's side. That night, she packed her bags and left.

"And that's how I ended up here," she said, getting up to refresh our drinks and turn the record over. The songs were short and snappy. We had blasted through side one in seemingly no time.

"So, what's your story?" she asked.

I paused, wondering what to say. I'd always vowed never to reveal anything about my true nature to anyone, but that had changed since Ben had come on to the scene. If it hadn't been for him, I would never have got to know Charlotte and I felt more comfortable around her than I had with anyone before.

Maybe it was because I felt the need for support, maybe I was emboldened because of the rum, I don't know. All I know was that at that moment in time I desperately needed someone to trust with my secrets and Charlotte seemed to fit the bill perfectly.

"I'm a time traveller," I blurted out.

"Sure," she said, looking sceptical.

Maybe this was a bad idea, I thought.

"Like Marty McFly?" she added.

"Nothing like that," I said. "OK, I should clarify. I can't travel through time, it's more of a reincarnation type thing. I can see the future because I've lived this life before."

"Maybe the Bacardi's gone to your head," she suggested.

"It has a bit," I said, and it was true. I was feeling more than a little tipsy. "How much rum did you put in this?"

"I always say if you're going to have a drink, have a proper drink," she replied.

"Well, that's probably what's loosened my tongue," I said. "But now I've started, I may as well tell you the whole story. It's not like we're in a rush to go anywhere, is it?"

"Come on then, H. G. Wells. Humour me."

I did just that, and over the next hour, as our afternoon grew increasingly alcoholic, I told her everything. It was such a relief to finally get it all off my chest.

At first, she looked cynical but that wore off as I told her more about all that had happened, from that day with Terry in the playground, right up to my encounters with Ben. When I described the alternate timeline where she had ended up shagging him in the student union office, I could see her becoming increasingly fascinated.

I finished off by telling her about the Devon train crash, just a few days away. When this happened, bang on schedule, she would have to believe me.

The rum was all gone by now, and through the cracked, single skylight in the diagonal, slanting roof, darkness had begun to fall.

"Do you believe me?" I asked.

"You've got a very vivid imagination, I'll give you that," she said, "but you haven't exactly painted a glowing picture of me, have you?"

"I'm only going on what he told me," I replied. "His words, not mine, and as we both know, his choice of vocabulary leaves a lot to be desired."

"So, in this alternate timeline, he got me pregnant, then I trapped him and ruined his life? Does that sound like me?" she asked, leaning in closer as she did.

I could sense her proximity and, just as in the library a few weeks before, there was a palpable feeling of sexual tension hanging in the air. But it was more dangerous this time. There was no fierce librarian to break us up, plus the small matter of half a bottle of rum which had lowered my inhibitions.

"No, it doesn't sound like you at all," I said. "Ben slagged you off to heaven, saying what an unfeeling bitch you were throughout the marriage. That's not what I'm seeing. I think he was the problem, not you."

The whole time I was talking, she was moving closer and I knew she was trying to seduce me. What was she looking for, deep down? Was it just sex, or comfort, love, and all the things she had been denied since her father had died? I didn't know, all I knew was that I was attracted to her and I didn't want to resist her advances.

I knew it was breaking all my rules, and I'm also ashamed to admit that by that point, I had forgotten all about Sarah. My passion for Charlotte, inflamed by the alcohol and the time we had shared, was overriding all rational thought.

This time when she leaned in to kiss me, I didn't resist. She got up and led me over to her tiny bed. The unkempt, unwashed bed covers didn't even register by then because nature had taken over.

Chapter Eight - Charlotte

All I had ever wanted was to feel wanted.

Until I was fifteen, I was. I know everyone says that they have the best dad in the world, but I truly did. No matter how busy he was with work, he always had time for me.

The first thing he did when he got home every night at 6pm was to come straight to me to ask how my day was. He also read to me every night when I was little, unlike some dads who preferred to spend their time in the pub.

Weekends and school holidays were full of happy moments, cycling down country lanes and swimming in the local river. They were idyllic, simple times. Dad and I shared a love of popular music and as the 1970s morphed into the 1980s, we got into The Clash, Squeeze, and many other cool bands of the time.

He was so different from some of my friend's parents who still thought Cliff Richard was the in thing. They hated punk. I was permanently banned from one house for asking if they had anything by The Sex Pistols at a birthday party.

My mother, on the other hand, was aloof and cold. She considered that her parental responsibilities had been fulfilled provided she had put a meal on the table and washed my clothes. She never showed any interest in anything I was into or anything to do with family life. She and Dad didn't seem to communicate much, either. She often appeared to be distracted, as if her mind were elsewhere.

Once I asked her why I didn't have any brothers or sisters. She just laughed and said, "there's not much chance of that happening unless you believe in the immaculate conception."

I was only about nine at the time so didn't understand what she meant by that. Of course, I do now and think she was totally out of order saying something like that to me.

Occasionally, Dad would be away for a couple of days on a business trip. One time, when I was in my early teens, I woke up late one evening to hear her talking on the phone in the hallway. I don't know who she was talking to, but I knew it wasn't Dad. She was saying "I love you," for a start and I had never heard her say that to him.

I was old enough now to be getting an inkling of how adult relationships worked. I came to realise that we didn't live in a cosy little world where every mum and dad loved each other.

I began reading books by Judy Blume and Sue Townsend, notably the Adrian Mole books. These gave me plenty of insight into grown-up issues.

Then, suddenly, and shockingly, Dad died of a heart attack. The horrific events of that day will be etched on my memory forever.

The traditional image of a heart attack as portrayed on screen is of someone clutching at their chest and gasping before collapsing. What happened to Dad was nothing so dramatic. It was far more shocking because of how mundane the circumstances were.

The three of us were sitting around, quite normally, having our Sunday dinner. As usual most of the conversation was between me and Dad, whilst my mother sat in stony silence. We were talking about the upcoming Live Aid concert and how amazing it would be to go if we could get tickets.

Then, without warning, he just keeled forward, his face falling directly into his plate of roast beef and Yorkshire pudding.

We thought he had just fainted at first, but when we couldn't rouse him, Mum phoned an ambulance while I increasingly panicked. I don't remember a lot of the detail because of my traumatic state, but one thing that does stick in my mind was that while I was screaming, she was remarkably calm. She didn't even seem upset.

It only took eight minutes for the ambulance to arrive, but it was eight minutes too late. He had suffered a massive coronary and died instantly for no apparent reason. He was forty-two years old.

It made no sense. He was incredibly fit and had run the London Marathon the year before. He was also still playing for a local football team. Eventually, we found out he had a rare heart condition that had gone undiagnosed because he had not been to the doctor for years. He had been at such a peak of fitness that he had never felt the need.

Less than six months later, Matt the twat moved in. He was charming, smooth, and good-looking. Life had to go on, said my mother, and she couldn't mourn my father forever. From what I could see she hadn't mourned him at all.

As for getting on with life, she was certainly doing that, for several hours a night by the constant sound of the wails coming from her bedroom. It hadn't taken her long to find a replacement– assuming that he hadn't been around all along. I suspected it was him she had been whispering sweet nothings to on the phone that time my father was away. For all I knew, they had been having an affair for years.

Her interest in me was at an all-time low. I was feeling increasingly surplus to requirements and retreated into my music, which became darker, reflecting how I felt inside. Night after night I listened to the melancholy musings of my new favourite bands who touched my soul in a way no-one in my real world could.

Over the next year, I transformed myself completely. I dyed my blonde hair black, the first step in a new monochrome version of me. My mother didn't even notice, or more likely, took no notice. Someone else was beginning to pay me attention, though, and not in a good way.

A few days after my sixteenth birthday I was in the shower, when unbeknown to me, someone sneaked into the bathroom. When I opened the shower door, I was shocked to see Matt standing right in front of me.

He looked me up and down appreciatively, almost licking his lips.

"Looking good," he said. "You're your mother's daughter alright."

"Get the fuck out!" I screamed, grabbing for a towel, desperate to cover my nakedness, cursing myself for not locking the bathroom door.

But he didn't get out and advanced towards me.

"Come on sweetheart, don't be like that. You knew I was at home today. You wouldn't have left the door unlocked if you hadn't wanted me to come in."

"I forgot!" I exclaimed.

"Course you did, you little tease. Don't worry, you're sixteen now, it's all legal. I'm a man, you're a woman. Well almost. Why don't you let me show you what being a woman is all about? I'm sure you've heard the noises your mother makes in bed."

"I can't bloody get to sleep because of it," I replied. "The two of you should show some consideration. I do have to get up for school in the mornings you know."

"Oh, yes, school," he replied. "You look so sexy in your uniform. I bet the boys at school would love to get their hands on you. Let me tell you, they wouldn't be able to please you the way I can. A real man like me can show you the ropes."

"You're disgusting," I exclaimed. "Get away from me."

"Come on," he said. "You know you want it," and to my horror, he leaned forward and tried to touch me between the legs.

No-one other than myself had ever touched me like that down there and this dirty, old pervert certainly wasn't going to be the first. I jumped back, switched the shower back on, grabbed the head and turned it directly on him, soaking his expensive Armani shirt. He was such a poser.

"You bitch," he shouted, dropping the false, charming persona he liked to portray.

Thankfully, he then backed off because by that point I was seriously fearing that he was going to rape me.

"Now get out," I shouted. "And don't think I won't tell Mum about this."

"She won't believe you," he said. "I'm the best thing that's ever happened to her. I make double what your old man earned, and I can give her multiple orgasms. He couldn't even give her one. You really should let me show you what you're missing."

"Over my dead body, you pervert," I screamed.

"We'll see," he said, mercifully heading back towards the bathroom door. "Sooner or later, I'm going to have you…"

And with that, he was gone, leaving me weeping in the bathroom.

I was determined that I was never going to let him touch me. I became remarkably adept at staying out of his way and never again forgot to lock the bathroom door. I also bought and installed a lock on my bedroom door.

Unfortunately, he was spot on about my mother not believing me. She was extremely horrible when I tried to explain what happened, dismissing my claims, and accusing me of lying. Then, to add insult to injury, she accused me of coming on to him!

I was left in no uncertain terms as to where I stood in the pecking order. This man was more important to her than her own daughter.

I stuck it out for a couple of years, avoiding the pair of them. I threw myself enthusiastically into the gothic scene, sneaking into The Dolly underage to see some great bands. I also worked hard at the college where I had gone to do my A levels, determined to make it in life. All the while I was counting down the days until my eighteenth birthday in November 1987.

As soon as that day came, I moved out. My father had left me a small trust fund that I wasn't able to access until I came of age. It amounted to a little over £5,000, and I was determined not to waste it.

I put down a deposit to rent the smallest room I could find in a student house and moved out, never to return. I didn't squander the rest of my savings. I was determined to make ends meet and got a job at the convenience store on the corner, selling cheap booze and cigarettes to other students.

In some ways, I was loving life. I had my independence, friends, I dressed the way I wanted, and I listened to the music I liked. But I was desperately lonely, and I had been ever since Dad had died.

I lost my virginity in the flat to one of the other students who lived in the house only a few days after I moved in. He was older, in his third year at Oriel, and I quickly realised he'd taken advantage of me when he introduced me to his girlfriend a few days later. Of course, he had conveniently neglected to mention her when he was charming me into bed. When his girlfriend showed up, he gave me a knowing glance that said, "keep quiet."

After that I drifted from boy to boy, getting plenty of sex but no love. What I really wanted was a boyfriend, someone I could call my own. I wanted a career but longed to settle down and be a mum, even at my tender age. Then I could be the best mother ever – to compensate for the lack of love my mother had given me.

Most of the boys I went with weren't other goths. There was this misplaced assumption that we were cold, depressed, and unapproachable, only mixing with our own kind, but that wasn't true in my case.

Sure, my two best girlfriends were goths too, but we didn't sit around gloomily thinking about slashing our wrists all day. We were more than happy to interact with other people if they accepted us for who we were.

I wanted to get to know as many people as I could which is why I entered enthusiastically into the student union movement. There wasn't a great deal of competition, so it was relatively easy to get elected on to the council and involved in college business.

I was also a regular visitor to The Duke at lunchtime, where my friends and I monopolised the jukebox. When I was asked to take part in some crazy drinking competition, I was all for it. It was another way of meeting people – and that's how I came to know Ben.

When I first saw him, he caught my eye. I knew he was a bit of a loudmouth, but he had a certain cocky confidence about him that I found attractive. He was also very beefy and looked like he worked out. I decided I would try and get his attention by giving him a run for his money in our drinking match.

What I hadn't expected was the despicable way he humiliated me in front of the whole pub. He was incredibly cruel and half of it didn't even make any sense. He seemed to be accusing me of things I was supposedly going to do in the future.

Then there was Thomas. He was kind, considerate and thoughtful. I hadn't taken much notice of him before the incident in the pub, but afterwards, I quickly warmed to him.

It was different from what I had felt towards Ben, an attraction borne out of respect and empathy rather than pure, physical attributes. I tried it on with him in the library, but he wasn't interested and suggested I would be better off with Ben.

It was an odd thing to say, but I didn't give it much further thought as I didn't see either of them again for several weeks. Then I bumped into Thomas in town and invited him back to my room. It was a wonderful, precious afternoon where we drank rum, laughed, listened to music, and told each other our life stories. It was the happiest I had been in ages.

Then he dropped a bombshell on me by claiming he could see into the future. I didn't believe a word of it at first, thinking he was some sort of fantasist, but he told a very convincing tale.

One thing he said that struck a chord with me was when he told me about an alternative timeline where I'd ended up with Ben. He explained that was why he had been so cruel to me that day in the pub. When I thought about it, I could almost hear Ben's voice echoing in my head.

You must be crazy if you think I'm going to be caught out a second time.

A second time. That resonated with me. It did fit the narrative. Thomas explained that my life was now following a different course from the one it should have taken.

I wanted to believe it all, I truly did. But what I wanted most of all right then, was to be close to him. Emboldened by the rum that I had drunk I launched myself at him and he put up little resistance.

Afterwards, we lay back and basked in the afterglow, cuddling up contentedly until we fell asleep. It was only early evening, and I awoke again an hour or two later. By then the mood had changed.

He was already up and out of bed, standing on one foot as he attempted to put a sock on the other in the cramped space beside the bed. He failed to keep his balance and toppled back on to the bed. I tried to grab him, eager not to let him get away.

"Come back to bed," I said. "You don't have to go yet."

"I do," he said. "We shouldn't have done that."

His whole demeanour was different. Where he had been loving and attentive before, looking into my eyes as we made love, now he was distant and wouldn't even make eye contact.

He may as well have slapped me across the face. Is this what all men did? Took their pleasure and then took their leave? It wasn't the first time.

"You're running out on me? Why?"

"This wasn't supposed to happen," he replied. "It's messing with the timeline."

"Oh, get real!" I said, genuinely annoyed now. "If you don't want me, have the guts to tell me, don't come up with pathetic excuses. You weren't worried about the timeline earlier when you were getting your end away, were you?"

"I guess not," he replied, sheepishly.

"You know what the saddest thing of all is? For a while there, I almost believed you."

"Everything I told you before was true," he insisted. "Watch the news on Thursday night. When that train crashes, you'll know I didn't make it up."

"Whatever you say," I replied, as he cast his eyes around the room. "Lost something?"

"My other sock," he said.

"Over there, in cobweb corner," I replied, pointing to the darkest and dirtiest part of the room.

"Yuck," he replied, as he picked up his discarded item of footwear, brushing the dust and cobwebs off it. "You really ought to clean this place up."

"And you ought to stop taking advantage of girls when they're drunk," I retorted.

"That's not fair," he protested. "You leapt on me, remember? And if I recall correctly, you were the one plying me with the rum, not the other way around."

"Yeah, well, I'll save my next bottle for a more deserving case," I replied.

I knew that I was upset and taking it out on him but why shouldn't I? He clearly couldn't wait to be gone. What was so wrong with me that every man rejected me, one way or another?

"Go on then, if you're going," I added. "But I'm not impressed. Not impressed at all!"

Pulling on his coat, he headed for the bedroom door.

"Take a good look at these," I added, flashing him my breasts as he turned back towards me. "Something to remember me by, as I doubt that you'll be seeing them again."

"There's no need for that," he said. "We can still be friends."

"I've heard that one before," I said. "You can see yourself out."

And that was the end of it, at least for the time being, as he walked out the door. I heard the floorboards creaking as he descended the stairs, and then he was gone. All I had left was a warm, wet feeling inside, and even that was beginning to fade.

The anger I felt at his departure wasn't so much at him, it was at the world in general. My craving to feel wanted had only been temporarily sated and now I felt more alone than ever. Right then, I wanted my dad so badly. None of this would ever have happened if he hadn't died.

I wrapped the quilt tighter around myself, desperate to cling to the little warmth that remained, but nothing could take away the cold, empty feeling that once again pervaded my soul. What did I have to do to make someone love me?

I ended up crying myself to sleep, as I had so many times in the past three years. Then, the next day, I dragged myself up and went back to work in the shop as usual. I saw and heard nothing of Thomas, but I hadn't expected to. He had made his position clear.

There was one footnote to this encounter that still needed to be resolved. A couple of nights later, I turned on my black and white portable TV to watch the *Six O'clock News*. Nicholas Witchell didn't say anything about a train crash, but I left the TV on, in case it wasn't reported until later.

It was a disappointing episode of *Top of the Pops* and then I fell asleep during *Tomorrow's World*, but I woke up in time for the next news bulletin just after 9pm. There was nothing about any train crash on there either.

I was on the early shift at the shop the following morning, which meant getting in and marking up the papers. With a sense of resigned inevitability, I scoured the headlines, and just as I had suspected there was nothing.

It feels wrong to feel disappointed because a train crash that would have killed dozens of people hadn't happened, but that's how I felt. I had wanted Thomas to be right. The idea of time travel being a real possibility had brought a flicker of excitement to my otherwise drab existence.

That hope had now been well and truly extinguished. Of course, time travel didn't exist. How could I have possibly imagined it did? It was a fantasy, just like my hopes that the few moments of pleasure I had shared with Thomas a couple of nights before might lead to something more.

Deflated, I started to put the newspapers on to the shelves. Thomas had lied to me, and now I had absolutely nothing to look forward to.

He had claimed he could see a different future.

But I couldn't see any future at all.

Chapter Nine - Ben

I'd only gone and done it!

Interfering with the timeline? Child's play. I'm a hero, even if no-one knows it because I've just saved ninety-eight people from plummeting to a watery grave. And where was that namby-pamby, Thomas, during all of this? Nowhere to be seen.

I knew a great deal about the rail disaster. Not only had it been headline news at the time, but before I left 2020, I had watched a documentary about it. One of the satellite channels had been running a series called *Transport Tragedies* and I loved anything like that. It explained the cause of the disaster in detail.

The driver had been going too fast, in stormy weather on a weak section of the track along the coastline that was long overdue for repair. I knew exactly where it would happen and when it would happen.

All I had to do was stop the train. This was going to be dangerous because the only realistic way I could do this was to be on board.

Was I really that crazy? I was planning to get on a train bound for disaster, just to prove a point. It's not like there was anything in it for me. I had to concede that Thomas had been right when he said that you cannot be rewarded for preventing a catastrophe that never happened.

I tried to think of an alternative but there wasn't one. There was no helpline to call for such things. The emergency services responded to incidents that had already happened, not wild predictions.

It appeared that the only way to contact British Rail in these primitive times was to write to them, and I couldn't see them taking any notice if they even read my letter. It would probably get lost among the thousands they received every day grumbling about the service.

I toyed briefly with the idea of phoning in a warning that there might be a dodgy package on the train. I swiftly dismissed that because the last thing I wanted was the anti-terrorist squad on my back.

I had no option but to be on the train, but I could take precautions that would ensure my safety even if my plan to stop the train failed. The footage from the documentary had shown that it was only the engine and the front three carriages that had gone off the tracks. They had fallen several metres from the cliffside onto the rocks below, bursting into flames before being swept away in the stormy waters.

All the deaths had occurred in those carriages with those in the rear far less affected. There were still plenty of minor injuries further back as people were thrown out of their seats with luggage flying everywhere. I would be caught in that if things went wrong, but I would survive.

I boarded the train at Reading, taking a seat in the rear carriage, and settled back to watch the world fly by. Once we were into Devon there were frequent glimpses of the sea from the picturesque line which ran along the coast.

I had calculated exactly where and when to exercise my plan, and I am pleased to say I got it spot on. Two minutes after we passed Starcross station, I got to my feet and pulled hard on the emergency cord.

I derived an immense amount of satisfaction from this act. Every time I had ever been on a train, I had felt a strong urge to pull the cord. The warning underneath threatening a fifty pound fine for improper use merely added to the attraction. I like breaking rules. An episode of *The Young Ones* I had seen in my impressionable youth had only heightened this desire.

I was shocked by how quickly the train stopped. It was remarkably like slamming on the brakes during an emergency stop in a car. The subsequent jolt caught everyone unawares, most notably a rotund lady in late middle age who ended up with a large portion of Victoria sponge plastered all over her face.

"What on earth do you think you are doing, young man!" she exclaimed in a hoity-toity accent. "Guard! Guard! Arrest that man!"

Unfortunately for me, a guard was already rushing along the carriage towards me, as the train ground to a complete halt. This was going to be interesting.

"It was him! He pulled the emergency cord!" screeched the tubby woman amongst the general din that had broken out. This included a baby screaming its lungs out and raised voices from various other mishaps around the carriage.

I didn't like the look of the guard, as he approached me in his uniform of dark blue waistcoat and cap. He was quite old, probably in his fifties, with a greying moustache, but looked like he meant business.

"Now what do you think you're playing at, lad! I think you'd better come along with me."

He grabbed me by my coat lapels and tried to drag me up the carriage. He was remarkably strong for an old geezer. Probably ex-army, by his demeanour.

"Get the hell off me," I said. "This is assault."

"Like hell it is," he replied. "I'm well within my authority."

"I've just saved all your lives!" I protested as he dragged me along the carriage, aware that all eyes were on me. There were looks of disapproval coming from all directions.

"Save it," replied the guard. "You're coming to the guard carriage with me. And you'd better have a bloody good explanation for pulling that cord."

"Do you get a kick out of upsetting kids," yelled a stressed-out young mum, who was trying to soothe the screaming baby.

"I'm going to be late for my holiday now," said another, older woman, who was travelling with two sulky looking teenagers.

"You'll get there a lot earlier than you would have if I hadn't pulled that cord," I replied.

"Come on," insisted the guard. "Move yourself."

"Alright grandad, I'll come quietly," I said. I was quite enjoying this and was looking forward to winding the old twat up a bit. He couldn't do anything to me.

In the guard's van, I was shoved roughly onto a makeshift seat made from an upside-down beer crate and given the third degree.

"Do you know how long we're going to be stuck here now? Do you?" demanded the guard, getting right in my face.

"A while, I would imagine, Colin," I replied, spotting a mug on the desk inscribed with the words 'Colin's tea'.

"That's Mr Barnett to you, lad," he said. "It's going to be a good half an hour. The driver is obliged to walk through and check the whole train before it can be restarted even though we know it was you who stopped it."

"Believe me, I've done you all a favour," I said. "Listen to that rain outside! It's not safe to be travelling in that at this speed."

I wasn't exaggerating. The wind was howling outside, and the rain was hammering down like hailstones on the carriage roof.

"Listen to me, you little know-it-all. I've been riding this line for nigh on fifteen years, and I've never heard of a train crashing because of a bit of rain! This isn't the A30, you know. These things run on rails."

"Rails which are old, and run around a bend next to a cliff with massive storm waves crashing against it?"

"I'm sure the driver knows what he's doing," said Colin. "He'll slow down if he deems it necessary."

"But he wouldn't have, that's the whole point. So, I took the decision out of his hands."

"I'll enjoy seeing you tell him that when he gets here."

"I will," I replied defiantly, and I did just that when he arrived a couple of minutes later.

"I drive at a speed appropriate for the conditions," he protested. He was young for a train driver, probably mid-twenties at a guess, fair-headed and slim.

"You look like a bit of a boy racer to me," I said. "I bet you've got a souped-up Vauxhall Nova at home with a spoiler on the back, haven't you?"

"That's Karen's car!" he protested. "And how do you know that anyway?"

"Just a lucky guess. I take it Karen's the missus?" I enquired. I bet you've even got one of those stickers across the top of the windscreen with your names on, haven't you? What is your name anyway? Is it Wayne? Oh, please let it be Wayne, that would make my day."

I couldn't remember what his name was. If it had been mentioned in the documentary, I must have missed it.

Colin had had enough of this and decided to assert his authority.

"Enough of this idle chit-chat," he declared. "There's a train full of people out there waiting to get to Cornwall for their holidays, and more doubtless backing up on the line behind us."

"It's not going to be much of a holiday in this weather," I remarked. "Still, it's better than being dead, I suppose,"

"That's enough of your lip," said Colin. "Now, you've got two choices. You can hand over the fifty quid fine right now and we'll throw you off at the next station. Or we can contact the police, get them to meet you off the train and you can take your chances with them."

"Don't sweat, Col," I said, knowing that level of familiarity would irritate him. I reached into my coat pocket, pulled out my wallet, and peeled off a wad of brown ten-pound-notes. These old notes were so much better than the twenty-first century, orange polymer versions. They felt like real money.

"Will tenners do you?" I asked as if I were handing out money like a bank clerk.

Trevor looked annoyed as I handed over the cash.

"You didn't think I was going to pay up, did you?" I said, enjoying his discomfort. "Oh, and I'll have a receipt if you please. We wouldn't want that money not being properly accounted for, would we? British Rail can do with every penny it can get, judging from what I've seen."

"Right, well I am off to get the train restarted," said the driver.

"Right you are, Steve," said Colin.

"Oh, you're not a Wayne then," I said. "That's a shame. Never mind. Now you remember what I said, Steve. Go careful on this stretch of the track in future."

"I'll remember that," he replied, before adding sarcastically. "Because I make a habit of taking advice from teenage boys who have never driven a train in their lives."

"Whatever," I replied. "It's your funeral."

Steve went off to get the train restarted and Colin was as good as his word, grabbing me by the scruff of the neck and unceremoniously dumping me on the platform in the rain at Newton Abbot.

"And never darken my train with your presence again!" he declared, as he slammed the door closed.

I was feeling rather pleased with myself. The train had stopped just short of the crash site, so when it restarted, we were going a fraction of the speed we would have been. I couldn't wait to get back to Oxford and rub Thomas's nose in it but decided to stay put for the night and go back the next day. Hopefully, I wouldn't be unlucky enough to encounter Colin on the return journey.

I wasn't bothered about having to hand over the fine. That was just a necessary expense I had incurred in my bid to prove my point and irrelevant to my long-term finances. Fifty quid would soon be worth about the same to me as a penny is to the average person.

I had raided my savings, cashing in a trust fund that had been set up by my parents for college. Unknown to them, I had taken out the lot, which amounted to around £1,500. I had already spent a chunk of it but was keeping the rest aside ready for the Grand National which was coming up the following weekend.

The race was the first leg in a planned betting coup which was going to set me up nicely for the years ahead. I knew all the Grand National winners and that Rhyme 'n' Reason would win this year at 10/1.

Back in Oxford, I didn't bother seeking Thomas out immediately. It was Easter, the college was shut, and I didn't want to brag too soon because I was a little concerned about something that he had said the last time we had met.

He had talked about alterations to the timeline, spreading out from where the changes had occurred. I couldn't see how something like me preventing a train crash could affect the result of a horse races hundreds of miles away a week later, but it was something I had to consider.

I was about to risk a thousand pounds, that had been saved by my parents to get me through college, on a horse. If this went wrong, I was seriously screwed.

OK, it wouldn't be the end of the world, but it would still be a huge setback. It would mean the timeline had been contaminated as Thomas had suggested so it wouldn't be as easy to take advantage of my future knowledge as I had hoped.

Even in that scenario, I still had a general idea of the way that the world would go and what the trends would be. Developments like the internet would still happen, of that I was sure. There would still be plenty of ways to take advantage of my foresight.

But I didn't want to wait that long. I wanted the easier path. I silenced the doubts in my mind and the temptation to lower my stakes or bet each way and resolved to put the whole thousand pounds on the nose.

On the morning of the race, I toured Oxford's betting shops, spreading my bet on Rhyme 'n' Reason around as many places as possible. I didn't want to draw attention to myself and a teenager trying to put a thousand pounds on a horse in one shop would certainly do that. In the space of three hours, I managed to visit twelve different shops, from Botley to Cowley.

I decided to watch the race in a Ladbrokes in town, which was packed to the rafters and full of atmosphere. It was a far cry from the soulless places these establishments would become in the future.

Rhyme 'n' Reason nearly fell at Becher's Brook on the first circuit and was left in last place. A feeling of dread sank through my body as if my blood were draining away. I felt sick, dizzy and the only thought in my head was "What have I done?" I wouldn't be able to explain this to my parents.

Could I justify it to myself? I knew that gambling brought people to the depths of despair, even suicide, but I didn't consider what I was doing was gambling in the traditional sense. It was the equivalent of insider dealing.

I was investing in the timeline and the odds were very much in my favour. It was like being offered odds of 10/1 on the toss of a coin. Even someone vehemently opposed to gambling would be tempted by that.

There was a lot at stake here, but it wasn't everything. I would still have a roof over my head if this went tits up, at least until my parents found out anyway. I would just have to regroup and come up with a new plan.

Fortunately for me, my fears were unfounded. Miraculously Rhyme 'n' Reason got going again and was second in the closing stages of the race. A horse called Durham

Edition was in the lead, but I remembered this now and knew my horse would collar him on the run-in. I had just won over £10,000 but this was only the beginning.

It was a nice amount of money, but hardly life-changing. I could have pocketed that and had a good time, but I was treating this like a business. I intended to reinvest my profits.

My actions in Devon had not affected the Grand National, so I felt more confident the following month. This would bring another major sporting event and a chance to land an even bigger prize.

The 1988 FA Cup Final was one that would live long in memory because of Wimbledon defeating the red-hot favourites, Liverpool.

Not only did I know Wimbledon would win, but I also knew both the score and the scorer of the winning goal. You got far greater odds for betting on these markets because there were more possibilities.

Wimbledon's team were known as the Crazy Gang, containing legendary players such as Vinnie Jones. Despite everything going to plan with Rhyme 'n' Reason's win, I wasn't about to go crazy and risk the lot.

The first thing I did was put back the money into the trust fund, so that was safe. I also stashed thousands in cash in my room, inside record sleeves. I figured that my parents, boring old squares that they were, would be highly unlikely to be interested in playing the latest Bon Jovi album.

The rest went on the football match, and when Lawrie Sanchez outwitted Bruce Grobbelaar to score the only goal of the game, I had made a small fortune. I now had over £100,000 to collect from the region's betting shops.

This proved remarkably difficult to secure from some outlets, who tried to make out I was underage, and the bets should be voided. When I produced my passport, clearly stating I was born in 1969, they had no comeback.

I asked for cheques this time as there was no way I was wandering around Oxford with that sort of money in my pocket, particularly in some of the less salubrious areas that you don't see on *Inspector Morse*. Once they were all in the bank and cleared, I was nicely set up for the future.

I spent wedges of cash like it was going out of fashion, most notably on fine clothes to befit my improved social status. Out went the cashmere jumpers and in came sharp, designer Italian suits. I could tell that I had impressed Jonty and Julian because their attitudes towards me improved considerably when we met for our weekly cocktails at Parkers. I made sure I flashed my cash at every opportunity, which also impressed the women. They were all over me.

Far from being pleased for me, my parents were being arseholes about it, demanding to know where I was getting my money from. That was easily solved. I packed my stuff and moved into The Randolph for a few days, before moving into a flashy, rented pad.

With that and the new sports car I also acquired, I was pulling the birds, left, right and centre. I don't mean fat, ugly ones like Charlotte, but fit models who appreciate a man with a decent car who treats them to champagne. It was a long way from halves of lager in The Duke.

I wasn't intending to stay in Oxford for much longer. I did not need to finish my course. Qualifications were meaningless to me. Who needed them, when money was so easy to come by? I had my sights set on the bright lights of London where I could get on and live the dream. Then, after that, who knows?

Before I left, there was one more thing I wanted to do. I wanted to show off to Thomas about how clever I was and how well I was doing. I had been tempted to do this right after the Grand National but had held off until my new lifestyle was well and truly in place. I wanted him to be green with envy when he saw how rich I was.

It would mean setting foot in that sordid little public house that all the plebs seemed to find such fun, but that was fine. I would probably be the best-dressed person ever to venture in there. By the end of May, I felt the time was right for my final visit. I knew they would all be in there on Friday lunchtime, so I settled on that as the best time to go.

It was a gorgeous sunny day, but not too warm, so I donned my £500 Armani suit, Ray-ban sunglasses, and rolled the soft top back on my sports car. There! I was all ready to lord it over the plebs. They would be so jealous!

I checked my look in the mirror and liked what I saw. Then I pulled out of the driveway of my luxury apartment block and roared down Woodstock Road. I was going at least 50mph and undercut a couple of cars by going into the bus lane, but who cared? I didn't.

I couldn't wait to get to the pub and see Thomas's face.

This was going to be so much fun!

Chapter Ten - Thomas

I didn't see Charlotte for a while after that afternoon in her flat and I didn't want to.

It wasn't because I didn't like her. It was quite the reverse and therein lay the problem. Firstly, I had broken the golden rule of not making major changes in my personal life. Secondly, and more importantly, I had felt genuine feelings towards her and that was dangerous. It felt like a betrayal of Sarah.

This hadn't happened before. I had slept with Simone and a couple of other girls without a pang of regret, justifying it as maintaining the timeline. Also, I hadn't cared much about any of them.

When I dwell on this it makes me feel shallow and I start to question my whole philosophy. Is it right to sleep with some girl just because I enjoy sex, on the pretext that it is part of a grand pre-destined scheme? Especially when I change that narrative when it suits?

It isn't acceptable and I should never have allowed the situation with Charlotte to develop. The most dangerous part was that I liked her so much. If I had been some normal person with no knowledge of the future, I could quite happily have started a relationship with her.

One of the most annoying elements of all this was that if Ben hadn't come on to the scene, none of this would ever have happened. Not only had he changed things, but he had also dragged me into the changes. Without his interference, nothing would ever have developed between Charlotte and me.

That's why I had to stay away from her because if I didn't, that life with Sarah would never happen. Even more importantly, Stacey would never be born.

I did my utmost to avoid Charlotte. I hadn't given her my number and she didn't know where I lived. I didn't go anywhere near The Duke, The Dolly, or The Gloucester Arms which I knew were the three main pubs she drank in. I also avoided the refectory and the student common room at college. This tactic worked well for several weeks.

Then, one day, she cornered me in the library. I was in a narrow area between two shelves right at the back, attempting to navigate the idiosyncrasies of the Dewey Decimal system. Without warning she appeared, crucifix swinging loosely around her neck. She was blocking the only way out so there was no avoiding a confrontation.

"I need to speak to you," she insisted loudly. "Why have you been avoiding me?"

"I haven't, I've just been busy," I said, without conviction, backing away straight into the shelf. This caused a large book to fall with a heavy crash onto the wooden flooring in the aisle behind.

"Oi!" shouted Joan, from the desk, not far from where we were standing. "What's going on over there?"

We heard the creak of her chair as she heaved her ample bulk up and began waddling over to investigate, half-moon glasses pitched on the end of her nose.

"Not right now," said Charlotte. "Meet me in the pub at lunchtime, in the pool room, after *Neighbours*. And you had better be there!"

With that, she was gone. I quickly whizzed round to the aisle behind, crouched down and picked up the book which turned out to be a dusty old tome entitled *The Russian Revolution*. It looked so ancient it might have been written at the time. As I got back up, I saw the fearsome shape of Joan looming over me.

"Sorry," I said, replacing the book on the shelf. "I accidentally knocked this off."

"Hmmm," she said, peering at me disapprovingly, before adding, "kindly be more careful in future, young man. I will not have students making unnecessary noise in this library."

"I will," I promised, as she turned around and began lumbering back to her desk, at a snail's pace.

Why had Charlotte come looking for me? Was she looking for a relationship? If so, why leave it this long? Did she think I might have changed my mind? I thought I had been clear enough that afternoon in the flat what my long-term plans were.

It was pointless speculating about her motives. The only way to find out was to go and meet her as requested. If I didn't, she would catch up with me eventually so I might as well get it over with.

I could hear the closing bars of the *Neighbours* theme tune playing as I pushed open the door to the pool room, with a pint of beer in hand.

She was waiting for me at one of the pub's many cheap, red tables, sipping cola through a straw. Unusually, there was no one else in the pool room so we would be able to speak freely. Straightaway, I set out to make my position clear.

"Look, Charlotte, what's this all about? I thought we both knew where we stood."

There was no preamble or pause to what she said next. She just dropped the bombshell right on me.

"I'm pregnant," she uttered, looking me straight in the eye.

This was the point where had this been a TV show, I would have dropped my pint on the floor in shock. But I had never seen that happen in real life. However, although my glass didn't crash, the rest of the world did around me.

"What?" I asked, in disbelief. "You can't be. How can this have happened?"

"Quite simply, really," she said, pointing rather crudely to my crotch and then to her own. "You put that in there."

Before I could respond, I was distracted by a cacophony from the window next to our table. The pool room faced the car park where some idiot was blasting his car horn repeatedly.

It seemed ridiculous to change the subject after her shocking revelation, but unable to think of any further response, it gave me a breathing space to gather my thoughts.

"What's going on out there?" I said, looking out through the grimy windows. It was some young guy sporting designer Ray-bans posing in an expensive, open-top Ferrari. It was like the one I had seen Tom Selleck driving in *Magnum P.I.*

He spotted me through the window and waved. Then, with a sinking feeling, I realised who it was.

"Oh, no, it's Ben," I said, as he leapt out of the car, revealing his flashy, designer suit and practically bounded up towards the pub's side door. "That's all we need."

Could this day get any worse? It was obvious he had come to show off to us, and I was right. He came straight into the pool room with a huge grin on his face. I had never seen someone so full of it.

"Yep, it's me!" he exclaimed. "Bet you're glad to see me, aren't you? What do you think of the wheels?"

"It's a bit vulgar if you ask me," said Charlotte. "But that suits you. Have you won the pools or something?"

Good old Charlotte. Whatever else was going on, at least I knew I could rely on her to put Ben down.

"Nothing so trivial," he replied. "This is what you get if you sign up to Maggie's philosophy. Haven't you heard of yuppies?"

"I have," said Charlotte. "Also known as arseholes. But they don't tend to drink in here."

"Well, they do today!" he said, reaching into his pocket and pulling out a wad of notes. "We've got something to celebrate. Me stopping that train crash for a start! I told you'd I'd do it."

"I thought you had made that up," said Charlotte, to me. "I watched the news all that night and there was nothing about it at all."

"That's down to me!" boasted Ben. "I saved nearly a hundred lives! I'm a hero! And now I'm rich. Have a look at this lot. Do you think that old git, Arthur, accepts fifty-pound notes?"

"He didn't earn that money in any sort of honest way," I said. "He cheated his way to it."

"What does it matter where it came from?" he asked. "Did I break any laws to acquire it? No. So wind your neck in, Saint Thomas. Now, what are you drinking? Come on, it's on me. I've got loadsamoney!"

Everyone had been overusing that catchphrase for months since Harry Enfield had popularised it and I was sick of hearing it. Especially from the likes of Ben.

"Not for me, thank-you," said Charlotte, rather formally. "I'm not drinking at the moment."

"Come on, it's a special occasion!" said Ben. "We're celebrating how much more successful I am than Thomas. How about a bottle of champagne? I'll treat you. That's assuming they sell it in here, of course. I can't imagine there's much demand for it in this dump. We might have to settle for three bottles of brown ale."

"I told you, I'm not drinking," she insisted.

"Why not?" asked Ben. "What's the matter with you? You're not on antibiotics, are you? You should have asked the doctor for the ones you can drink with. I always do."

"If you must know, I'm pregnant!" she blurted out.

I had hoped she wasn't going to say that. It took a second or two for it to sink in, and then his grin grew wider than ever. This was rapidly turning into the worst day ever.

"Oh…my…God," he said deliberately leaving dramatic pauses between each word. Then he looked at each of us in turn, first her, then me, then her again. I knew exactly what he was thinking and what he was going to say next and it was nothing to do with any sort of premonition.

"Is it his?" he asked, with glee. "Oh, please tell me it's his."

He was overexcited like a kid on an overdose of e-numbers.

"Yes, it is," she said.

I cast her a look of disapproval for dropping me in it. He was going to have a field day with me now.

"Awesome!" exclaimed Ben, turning to me. "This is absolutely and without doubt the best news ever! After all that lecturing you gave me about the timeline, and how I had to fulfil my destiny with Charlotte!"

He turned back to her, to continue his rant.

"Did he tell you about that?" he asked. "How he begged me to shag you and get you pregnant to ensure he could be with his precious wife he thinks he's going to meet in the future. A wife he hasn't even met yet, I should add! But I wouldn't play ball, so what does he go and do? Knocks you up himself!"

"Excuse me, I did play a part in all this," said Charlotte. "I'm not some plaything that you two can pass around between you. It was my choice to sleep with Thomas and I'm glad I did. I wouldn't want an egotistical, selfish man like you to father my child under any circumstances."

"Don't kid yourself!" said Ben. "You're a mere pawn in the game. You don't have the insight into the future that we have. For example, you may be young and attractive now, but I know you're going to turn into a boring, fat, middle-aged cow. Why do you think I didn't shag you? Because I didn't want to get lumbered."

"You're bang out of order, Ben. You've no right to talk to her like that!"

"He can't help it," said Charlotte. "He's a classic narcissist. He doesn't care about other people's feelings. He did me a favour that day he knocked me back. It's me that's had the lucky escape, not him."

"You don't have any choice in this!" exclaimed Ben. "You were all over me that day of that drinking match. If I hadn't blown you out that would be my baby in there now. And don't think he's going to stick around to play happy families with you. He's got other plans, and they don't include you. You're on your own, love, just another single mother who should have been more careful who she opened her legs for."

"Is that true, Thomas?" she asked, looking me right in the eye, again. I had well and truly been put on the spot.

I broke her gaze, looking down towards the floor. I was giving out all the wrong body language and knew I had to say something quickly, but what? I'd barely had time to digest the news she was pregnant, let along figure out what I was going to do about it.

"I need time to think about it," I said, weakly. "This has all come as a bit of a shock."

"He doesn't want you, it's obvious!" crowed Ben, determined to heap as much misery upon Charlotte as he could. "At least I stuck by you in the other timeline, much to my regret. He won't!"

Again, she looked across at me, with a searching look on her face, but I didn't know what to say. This was a horrible situation and Ben wouldn't let up.

"You want to get rid of that baby because if you don't it's going to be single motherhood and a life on benefits for you. Oh, but you won't, will you? You don't believe in abortion. Or so you claim. That's how she trapped me the first time around."

That was it, I couldn't let him talk to her like this any longer.

"That's enough!" I shouted, trying to sound as tough as I could. It wasn't something that came naturally to me. "Leave her alone."

I hadn't expected this to work and it didn't. He came over and stuck his face right in front of me. He was invading my personal space to the extent that his eyes were burning into mine, no more than six inches away.

"Make me," he uttered, softly. This was considerably more menacing than it would have been if he had shouted it. Charlotte had called him a narcissist, but I was seriously worried that it was a psychopath we were dealing with here.

I knew I couldn't make him, so I just backed away. This probably looked incredibly weak to Charlotte, but I had to get away from this situation. Weak or not, I couldn't leave her behind at his mercy.

"Come on, we're leaving," I said, offering her my hand which she eagerly took as I pulled her up from the chair. I wasn't holding her hand for romantic reasons, I just needed to get her safely out of there, but Ben, of course, seized on my gesture.

"Ah, how sweet, Mummy and Daddy holding hands," he said. "Off to choose a cot, are we?"

"Ignore him," said Charlotte, who was showing plenty of resilience considering how horrible he had been. "He's just a sad, pathetic creep who's bought a sports car to substitute for his tiny dick."

There I was thinking about protecting her from him, but she was proving much stronger than me. I could see her latest comeback had rattled him as his grin rapidly disappeared. The insult had hit home.

I wish I'd had the guts to stand up to him, but I knew he'd make mincemeat of me in a proper fight. At least he couldn't hit a woman and a pregnant one at that. I assumed he wouldn't, anyway. There was no real way of knowing what he was capable of.

"Screw you," he said, as we left the pool room. "I'd say have a nice life, but I know you both won't. I, on the other hand, am going to have an amazing life! Bye, losers!"

The door swung shut behind us, and mercifully, he was out of earshot. We headed straight for the side door and out into the car park. I was acutely embarrassed when I realised that I was still holding her hand. I pulled it away, rather too quickly.

"You don't get off that lightly," she said. "We still need to have that talk, but I've got a little job to do first."

Ben's Ferrari was parked directly opposite the room we had just been in. She looked across to the window, but there was no sign of him looking out. Perhaps he had gone to get a drink because he wasn't behind us either.

"Come on," she said, removing her crucifix from her neck and running across to the car, as fast as she could in her heavy, black boots. Gripping the top of the crucifix hard, she ran the base along the driver side from the bonnet to the petrol cap. It made a sound akin to chalk on a blackboard as it gouged a deep wound into the paintwork.

Then she went round to the bonnet and crudely scratched the word 'Twat' across it.

"That'll teach him," she said, with a satisfied grin on her face, as she completed her desecration of the expensive vehicle. "Now let's get out of here."

She led the way back across the car park towards the college and I trailed behind a little, in admiration at her act of vandalism. Ordinarily, I would have considered doing something like this to such a classic vehicle to be sacrilege, but this was Ben we were talking about here. He deserved it.

I had enjoyed the moment, but despite the temporary distraction, the news of Charlotte's pregnancy was weighing heavily on my mind. I wasn't going to get any insights to help me with this one, because it hadn't happened in my other lives. I was flying blind this time.

What the hell was I going to do? I was going to have to make some sort of decision quickly.

"We'll go in here," said Charlotte, dragging me into the refectory. It was mercifully quiet, as lunch was finished and most of the students that had bothered to come back from the pub were heading into their lectures.

We walked over to the far side of the room to one of the four-person booths, where we were able to talk undisturbed. I waited for her to sit down, then sat diagonally opposite. It seemed less confrontational to talk at an angle rather than directly across.

"So, what's the plan?" she asked. "Are you going to stand by me?"

"That's a little old-fashioned, don't you think? What if I say no? Is your father going to march me up the aisle with a shotgun?"

"I can't believe you've just said that!" she exclaimed. "You know he's dead! I poured my heart out to you about that and you've forgotten already! Were you even listening or just pretending to care to get a shag?"

"Shit, I'm so sorry," I said, feeling my cheeks turning a rich, crimson colour. I had well and truly put my foot in it.

"It was a stupid thing to say," I added. "All this has been a lot to take in and it was just the first thing that came into my head. Of course, I hadn't forgotten about your dad."

She seemed to accept this and changed the subject.

"OK, it was a slip of the tongue. I'll let it go – this time. Now, look, Thomas, I'm not going to make any secret of this. I like you. In fact, it's probably more than that. We get on, we like the same music, and we were good together. That afternoon we spent together was the happiest day I've had since before my dad died. We could make this work."

She was making a persuasive argument, and under normal circumstances, I would certainly have considered it.

"Charlotte, I'm sorry. I like you too, but I explained my position before. I've got someone waiting for me in the future, and a child who won't be born if I don't fulfil my destiny."

"Sod the future! That's ten years away. I need you now. You don't have to stick rigidly to what you did in your other life. You've already broken your own rules by sleeping with me. And what about our baby? Was this not supposed to be born? What do you want me to do about that? Do you want me to have an abortion? Because I tell you now, I won't. I want this baby, and I'm going to have it, with or without your help."

"I will help you," I said. "But we can't be together."

I hated myself for saying these words. I was breaking her heart and what's more, I was breaking mine too. The new baby had changed everything. Wasn't the unborn child just as important as Stacey? This was an impossible situation.

"Please, Thomas, at least consider it. You don't have to marry me or anything. We could try having a relationship and see how things go. If it doesn't work out and you decide in ten years from now that you still want to go and be with Sarah, I won't stand in your way."

"How can you say that?" I asked. "You don't know how you're going to feel then. A huge amount can happen in a decade. And what sort of man would I be if I did that anyway? Stringing you along, giving you false hope, then abandoning you?"

"Maybe you would grow to love me – to love both of us," she said, putting her hand on her stomach.

"I can't do that to you, Charlotte. It wouldn't be fair. But I promise I will help you. I will be your friend. I'll be part of the baby's life, and I'll provide for it. Do you know how Ben got so rich so quickly? He knows the future and he can make money from it. I can do the same. You and the baby will want for nothing."

"Except you," she said, a single tear emerging from the corner of her eye, and running down her pale, white face.

"I'm not the one, Charlotte. But you will find someone. Whatever happens, take solace from this. You are still going to have a far better life than the one you would have had with Ben."

"Well, when you put it that way," she said, cracking a half-hearted smile."

"There, see, it's going to be OK," I said. "Do you want a hug?"

"Please," she said.

I got up and slid in next to her on the other side of the booth putting both my arms around her as she rested her head on my shoulder.

It was an action that made me feel protective towards both her and the growing life inside her. For a moment, I seriously wondered if I was doing the right thing. Part of me wanted to be with her, but I knew it would never be enough. I would never stop dreaming about Sarah.

Charlotte deserved better than that. It might seem like I was doing the dishonourable thing now, but I would look after her. And what I'd said before was true. I was certain she would get a better life than the one she would have had with Ben.

As for me, I'd messed the timeline up good and proper, but at least it was still on a local basis. Hopefully, Sarah would be going about her business in Swansea right now, completely unaffected by anything that was going on here.

It was almost a decade now until the day we would meet for the first time, and even the events of today couldn't stand in the way of that.

Three days later, a train crashed in the same spot as the one Ben had prevented should have done. 126 people were killed, more than would have been the case before. He hadn't saved any lives at all; he had caused more deaths.

I was seriously worried about what he might do next.

Chapter Eleven - Thomas

Ten years had passed since the day Charlotte had told me she was pregnant.

Despite my initial reticence, things had worked out remarkably well.

I had been good to my word and done all I could to support Charlotte and be a good father. I couldn't give her the relationship she craved, but that became less of a problem over time.

What we had morphed into a close friendship, that grew stronger after she gave birth to our son just after Christmas 1988. I was by her side when she gave birth, and felt overwhelming, protective feelings towards my firstborn. We named him Jack, after Charlotte's late father, and from the start, I loved him as much as I imagined I would one day love Stacey.

All my previous hang-ups over timeline disruption went out of the window. The feelings and emotions that fatherhood brought far outweighed such considerations. This baby was mine, my flesh and blood. How could I ever have imagined that anything could be more important than that?

The help I gave Charlotte went way beyond throwing money at her to assuage my guilt at us not being together. That was what many absent fathers did and those were the better ones. Others washed their hands of their unwanted children completely, refusing to even acknowledge their existence. I could not understand how any man could be like that and I knew that I never would.

I was doing well enough financially to help her get out of her tiny, attic room. I put down a deposit for her to rent a lovely, airy modern flat in Headington.

I wasn't rolling in cash like Ben with his Ferrari, but I was doing well enough. He and I were making our money in the same way – betting on the outcome of sporting events we knew the outcome of, but I wasn't as greedy as him. I just took what we needed.

Charlotte was keen to continue her education and train as a nurse. I encouraged her in this, doing my share of the childcare and even arranging for a part-time nanny to give her the independence she needed.

I don't know the full story of what course her life would have taken in the other timeline, but I can't imagine it being pleasant. I doubted she would have had much support from Ben. Yes, he had stood by her by marrying her, but that was probably as far as it went.

In that other reality, he probably left her to do all the cooking and cleaning, surrounded by nappies, like a downtrodden housewife. I doubt he ever gave a moment's consideration to the idea that she might have ambitions of her own.

Often Charlotte and I spent time together, with me frequently staying over at the flat in the spare room. I sensed that she still wanted me, but I was careful never to let us become intimate again.

I must confess that I still felt a great deal of warmth towards her. I was tempted on more than one occasion to rekindle things but stuck to my guns. My dreams of Sarah were growing stronger over time and I still felt an unwavering conviction that my destiny lay with her.

I had come clean to my parents about getting Charlotte pregnant. After their initial anger and disapproval, their stance softened as they grew to love their grandson. They also became very fond of Charlotte, practically adopting her. I never met her mother and the notorious pervert, Matt. Charlotte remained completely estranged from them and didn't even tell them about Jack's existence.

My parents couldn't understand why I wouldn't get together with her and live happily ever after. Their constant badgering about it got so bad that eventually, I had to move out and get my own place. They immediately converted my old bedroom into a nursery, and before long Charlotte and Jack were spending more time there than I did.

My parents didn't stop devising schemes to try and get Charlotte and me together, and in the spring of 1990 announced that they wanted us all to go on a family holiday to Greece. It seemed we didn't have much choice, as they had already booked it. I was considerably irked when pressing my parents about the sleeping arrangements. It was clear that the layout of the villa would require Charlotte and me to share a room.

Even so, I was prepared to go along on the holiday, intending to sleep on the sofa. Then, a couple of weeks before we were due to depart, I started having dreams about meeting a middle-aged man with a strange device outside the Ratcliffe Camera in Oxford.

The man's name was Josh, and he was a time traveller. The dream suggested I had arranged to meet him at a certain place and time. It was written on a scrap of paper with my name on it, and a certain place and time. That was 6th August 1990 at 5pm at the Radcliffe Camera in Oxford. Unfortunately, this date was right in the middle of the holiday.

If Josh knew the secrets of how to travel through time, then this could be my one opportunity to find out why I was living this strange life. There was no way I could miss this meeting and that meant I was going to have to make an extremely unpopular decision. I was going to have to skip the holiday.

As you can imagine, that went down like a lead balloon. I tried to make some excuse about not being able to get out of work, but it didn't wash. Charlotte was inconsolable but that was nothing compared to the fury that my parents unleashed when I told them. I could not tell them why, so I made up some lame excuse about work commitments.

"Your son's only just begun walking, and you're going to miss his first holiday?" said my mum.

"What sort of father are you?" added my dad.

In the end, I compromised. The holiday was for two weeks and the date with Josh wasn't until the first day of the second week. I would go for a week and then fly back which wasn't too difficult to organise. There was still rather a lot of disgruntlement from the family, but they ultimately accepted the compromise.

The day before we flew to Greece, I had the misfortune to run into Ben again. I had not seen him since the day Charlotte had keyed his car. I had been surprised by this as I had expected him to keep popping up like a bad penny to lord it over us. That was the sort of thing he seemed to revel in.

I was walking past the front of the Randolph Hotel when he came out with a gorgeous supermodel on his arm. He was dressed even more ostentatiously than the last time I had seen him, having acquired a Rolex and various other bling since then. Quite frankly, he looked ridiculous.

She had long, blonde hair, an expensive-looking red cocktail dress, and looked like she had stepped straight out of a Hollywood movie.

"Oh, look who it isn't!" exclaimed Ben, turning to his companion. "Cindy, this is the loser I was telling you about earlier. What a coincidence."

"Pleased to meet you," she said, in a strong American accent, giggling as she did. She was every bit the stereotypical dizzy, rich bimbo. Although she was pencil slim, she had an impossibly huge cleavage that couldn't be real.

"Cindy's the daughter of a film director," said Ben. "He's nearly as rich as I am. I met her in L.A. at a party at the Playboy Mansion."

"They let you into the Playboy Mansion?" I asked incredulously.

"Oh, you can get anywhere, if you've got money, right, darling?" he said, crudely pinching his airhead girlfriend's arse.

Much as I despised Ben, his arrival was timely.

"Listen, Ben, I need to talk to you. It could be to your advantage."

I was expecting a load of abuse in return, but he was surprisingly polite. Perhaps Cindy was having a calming influence on him.

"Sure, it would be great to catch up again!" he said. "I've got so much to talk about."

"Brag about, more like," I said.

"Of course," he said. "Would you expect any less?"

He reached into his breast pocket and pulled out a black, leather wallet, embossed with what looked like real gold. He opened it, pulled out a gold credit card and handed it to Cindy.

"Here you go, sweetheart, the boys need to talk. Be a good girl and go and buy yourself something nice. I'll meet you back at the hotel in an hour."

"Sure thing, honey pie," she said, taking the cash and heading off into town.

"I've got her well trained," he boasted. "They'll do anything if you're loaded. I've had loads like her."

"Still the same old misogynistic, Ben, eh?" I asked.

"I still don't know what that word means," he replied.

"It shows," I said. "Come on let's go in here and have afternoon tea."

Afternoon tea in the Randolph was a delightful experience on any occasion. Even the dubious company couldn't spoil my enjoyment of the delicious food on offer. For the first ten minutes, I listened as Ben boasted about how rich he was and all the things he had done since he had last seen me.

"Oh, yeah, so broads like Cindy are ten a penny," he said. "Normally I would have got bored of her by now but if I play my cards right, she might be able to get me into the movies. Having money's great, but I want fame too!"

"You used to say birds, not broads. You've been spending too much time across the pond."

"I go all over the world, mate. Did I mention I had a private jet?"

"A couple of times," I said, reaching across to the sumptuous array of food on the three-tiered cake stand in front of us. I helped myself to a triangular, smoked salmon sandwich with the crusts cut off.

"It's awesome!" he continued. "I can go wherever I want, whenever I want. It's so much better than travelling first class on one of those grotty, little airlines."

Ignoring the sandwiches, he went straight for the cakes, picking out a sumptuous looking slice of Victoria sponge.

"What bring you back to Oxford?" I asked.

"I'm here for a wedding," he said. "Remember Jonty and Julian? They were the two chaps you embarrassed me in front of in Parkers a couple of years ago. Well Julian's getting married, the stupid twat. They invited me, so here I am."

"To show off, no doubt?"

"Hey, if you've got money, you may as well flaunt it. Jonty used to make a big deal about how much money he had. I think it's only fair I return the favour now I've got way more than him."

"You must be a really popular guy," I said, sarcastically.

"Actually, I am," he said. "Everybody loves me in L.A."

"They love your money," I replied. "You would be a complete nobody in their world without it."

"Whatever. Who cares? I'm living the dream. Anyway, what did you want to talk to me about? Cindy will be back soon, and I'll be wanting to take her back up to the room to bang her. Have you ever had sex with a supermodel? No, of course, you haven't."

I told him about my visions of Josh, and how I planned to meet him and suggested he should come along too. I spoke eagerly, but it was clear from his demeanour that he didn't share my enthusiasm.

"I honestly believe that this could be the guy who sent you back here. The device you described sounds exactly like the one I can see in my dream. Don't you see what this means? You can get home!"

"Get home!" he exclaimed. "Why the fuck would I want to get home?"

"Because it's the right thing to do," though I already knew what the response would be. When had he ever done the right thing?

"Look at it from my point of view," he said. "I'm twenty years old and already a billionaire. I'm sleeping with some of the most beautiful women in the world and I'm about to become a famous film star. What could possibly possess you to think that I might want to go back to the miserable life I had in 2020? You can go and meet this guy if you like but count me out."

"I take it that's a no, then?"

"Of course, it is!" he said. "He might send me back. And let me warn you now, don't even think about telling him about me. You weren't, were you?"

"It had crossed my mind," I replied.

"Who the hell do you think you are? You've no right to interfere in my life. Ever since I met you, you've been trying to tell me what I can and can't do. Well, let me warn you, I don't take that from anyone. With the sort of money that I've got, it would be extremely easy to make you disappear. Do I make myself clear?"

So, he was threatening me now. It didn't come as any surprise. There was no point in pursuing it further.

"Fine, don't come then," I said. "I just thought I should offer you the opportunity that's all. Go back to your shallow life and have sex with your plastic girlfriend because it's all meaningless. At least I'm staying true to my principles and when I finally meet Sarah, it will all have been worth it."

"Staying true to your principles? By shagging that slapper and getting her up the duff? I'm sure Sarah will be hugely impressed by that."

"She's not a slapper," I said. "She's a lovely person with a lot of potential in life, but I doubt you ever saw that."

"If by potential, you mean lying around on the sofa, eating chocolate and getting fat, then sure she has," he said.

"Perhaps if you had allowed her the chance to make something of her life rather than chaining her to the kitchen sink, she might have been a completely different person."

"Give it a rest, mate!" exclaimed Ben. "Do you have any idea how preachy you sound?" If you think Charlotte's so wonderful, why don't you marry her yourself? Oh no, I forgot, that would mess things up with your precious Sarah, wouldn't it? That's all a fantasy, mate. Why don't you try living in the real world?"

The conversation was going nowhere, so it was a relief at that point when Cindy walked into the room.

"Hey, sweet cheeks, look what I got!" she said, excitedly, reaching into a white plastic bag with a depiction of the dreaming spires on it. She pulled out a T-shirt with a similar design to the bag. It had the logo *Oxford University* emblazoned prominently across the top and she held it up in front of her impossibly large cleavage.

She seemed completely oblivious to the toxic atmosphere in the room but from what I had seen of Cindy, that didn't surprise me. To put it bluntly, she was all tit and no brain. Never would a T-shirt advertising Oxford University be worn by a more inappropriate person.

"That's lovely, my dear," said Ben, clearly completely uninterested by her tacky purchase. "I'm glad you're back. We're done here – aren't we?" He looked across at me with a look that made it clear that we were.

"It looks that way," I said, resigned to the fact that attempting to reason with Ben in any way was utterly pointless.

"Don't look so glum, mate. Here, you can have the rest of this food on me. It's the least I can do. Come on Cindy, I think we should go back up to our room. I want to see you try on your new t-shirt. Before you take it off again, of course."

"Ooh, Ben, you are naughty," she said, giggling.

She was like something out of a bad 1970s comedy film.

"You love it," said Ben, before turning back to me and saying, "have a nice life, loser."

I ignored him. If he wanted the last word, he could have it. I didn't care anymore. I had let him get the better of the exchange and he knew it.

He headed towards the door, with Cindy hanging off his arm, pausing only to tell the impeccably dressed maître d' to charge the large pile of food left in front of me to his room.

I had been dining with the devil, but I wasn't going to get all precious about it. Good food shouldn't go to waste, no matter who had paid for it, so I started on the scones, slathering them generously with jam and cream. When the maître d's back was turned, I wrapped a couple of cakes in napkins and stuffed them into my jacket pocket. They would make a nice treat for Charlotte and Jack later.

A few days later I flew out to the Greek Islands, where I spent a wonderful week with the family. My parents spent the whole time trying to create romantic scenarios for Charlotte and me to rekindle our passion. Inspired by the film *Shirley Valentine*, they even went as far as attempting to recreate the scene with the table on the beach at sunset.

It was tempting, I must admit. Who wouldn't feel amorous in such a setting, especially after a few shots of Metaxa? I was determined to stick to my plan, though. There would be other holidays, but I only had one chance to meet Josh. And despite Ben's threats, I wasn't going to stay quiet. Josh was my one hope of putting a stop to him.

My insistence on leaving halfway through the holiday did not go down well. Jack was starting to talk and when he asked, "where are you going, Daddy?" it nearly broke my heart.

It was a race against time to get back to Oxford, on a series of boats, planes, and buses. I made it to the Radcliffe Camera with moments to spare. Britain was sweltering in a heatwave and I was exhausted and thirsty, but it would all be worth it if I could get the answers I sought.

I could picture the man I was to meet as clear as if he were standing right in front of me, right down to his clothes.

All I had to do was spot him. It was high summer and there were crowds of tourists everywhere.

I searched desperately amongst the jabbering, phototaking mob, but couldn't see him. Perhaps he would come and find me. I sat down on the steps, close to a young, blonde girl and a guy in a denim jacket taking turns to swig from a bottle of white wine.

Then I waited. And I waited some more. The crowds thinned, the couple moved on, and afternoon turned to evening. It was still baking hot. I wanted to go and grab a drink, but I couldn't risk missing him. But there was still no sign.

By the time the sun started to set, I had to accept that he wasn't coming. I had cut my holiday short for nothing. Dejected, I trudged to The Turf Tavern for a couple of pints and then went home.

Why hadn't he been there? My premonitions were rarely wrong, and I had been so certain about this one. I had not even considered the possibility that he might not turn up. Was it something I or Ben had done to alter the timeline? Did I need to accept that we had messed around with things too much and now my visions had become unreliable?

Or was it something to do with Josh himself? He was a time traveller and probably didn't stick to the schedules of ordinary people. This world wasn't identical to the one I had lived in before. Perhaps he had turned up, but only in that other universe.

I tried to remember more about my meeting with him in my previous life. All I could recall from my dreams was his face, and him talking about travelling in time before showing me the device he called his tachyometer. Try as I might, I couldn't dredge up any more details than that.

This whole venture had been a complete waste of time. The next morning, pissed off at the whole situation, I made my way down to Gatwick, got myself on a flight back to Corfu and a boat back to Paxos.

By the evening, I was back on the square in Gaios, enjoying drinks with my family. They were delighted at my unexpected return. As for Josh, well I was just going to have to forget about him and manage by myself, just as I always had.

The years rolled by, and I began a career in the retail trade, following the path of my previous life. I started as a newsagent, getting up at stupid o'clock in the morning to get the papers ready for the local lads to deliver. I also bought my first car, a rusty old British Leyland Maxi.

I could have afforded better, but I had dreamt about this car so thought I had better stick with it. I had deviated off course enough already and I wasn't driven by a desire to show off with fancy motors like Ben.

A couple of years after our holiday in Greece, Charlotte met someone. Part of me was happy for her because I didn't want her to mope around after me forever.

His name was Darren, and he was an affable, though rather boring chap, who worked in a building society. I must admit feeling a pang of jealousy, but it was more to do with Jack than Charlotte. He would always know I was his dad, but there would now be another man living with his mother and involved in his upbringing.

Again, I found that I was doing an awful lot of soul searching in the small hours, wrestling with one philosophical debate after another. Had I chosen the right path? Was I banking too much on Sarah, who could turn out to be an elusive pot of gold at the end of a rainbow? Josh hadn't been where he was supposed to be. What if she wasn't either?

My career in retail progressed as I got a supervisor position in a supermarket. There, I made friends with a chap called Nick who quickly became my best friend and drinking buddy.

I moved out of my rented place into a new house on the Greater Leys estate. All the furniture was black ash, which was the in-thing at the time. I got the biggest TV on the market complete with a satellite dish and Sega Mega Drive. To put the finishing touch to my new bachelor pad, Nick and I converted the breakfast bar into a real bar, complete with beer pumps and optics.

My walls were lined not with literary tomes, but shelves and shelves of records and videotapes. The entire collection of Star Trek videos took up two shelves alone. That was a lot of storage space in what was quite a small house. They certainly liked to build compactly on these new estates.

Some weekends Jack would come to stay, sleeping in my room while I took the sofa bed in the lounge. Other weekends, I just let life take me where my instincts led me, and frequently this was various women's beds. I seemed to have an incredibly high sex drive and saw no reason to deny myself experiences I would have had anyway.

I usually knew when I met a woman that I was going to end up sleeping with her because I could foresee it. If I didn't get any such hints, then I knew nothing would ever happen between us. It was like having a personal dating radar. The amount of time I saw other people wasting in pursuit of liaisons that would never go anywhere was enormous. Nick was particularly bad at this, always going after the wrong women.

I didn't see or hear from Ben for several years after that day we took afternoon tea together. Then, in 1995, he was suddenly in my face wherever I went.

He had emerged as one of the stars of a hot new sitcom from America that had become a huge hit. It had been imported into the UK, where it was being advertised by Channel 4 on billboards everywhere. It seemed that Cindy had been as good as her word and got him into the acting world.

I forced myself to watch the predictably awful sitcom. Not long after that, he appeared on *Parkinson*. I tuned in, wondering how much the fame had gone to his head.

I had been expecting his usual arrogance but was disappointed. He came across as quite sincere, playing the local boy made good role. He had got used to handling the media over in Hollywood. I wasn't fooled for a moment because I knew this was all an act. Here was one leopard that would never change its spots.

After the *Parkinson* interview, I went out of my way to avoid the media, particularly gossipy tabloids, in which he seemed to feature almost every day. I got on with my life and the following year was one of the best yet.

The music was the best it had ever been. Britpop was at its height, and I couldn't get enough of Blur, Suede and Lush. The height of that summer was the Euro '96 football tournament. I knew in advance that England would lose on penalties against Germany, but it didn't stop me enjoying the wonderful atmosphere that pervaded across Britain that summer.

1996 gave way to 1997, a notable year, in which I foresaw a couple of notable events – a change of Government after eighteen years of Tory rule, and the death of Princess Diana. These were all things I knew had happened before, so the timeline seemed to be staying on track.

My fears that Ben might interfere in world events had proved unfounded. It appeared that he had made his point by stopping the first train crash and was now too busy enjoying himself for any further interventions.

As I celebrated Hogmanay with Nick on a trip up to Edinburgh, I knew I was entering the year in which I would finally meet Sarah. Up until this point, I had resisted the temptation to pop down to Swansea to observe her from afar, but as summer approached, the desire became too great.

I wasn't intending to approach her, but I just wanted to reassure myself that her life had also stayed on track. There was no point me going to Ibiza if she wasn't going to be there.

About two weeks before she was due to fly out, I drove down to Swansea one sunny Saturday afternoon. I parked my car outside the flat she shared with her friend, Sam, with a bag of doughnuts and a flask of coffee for company. I was all set for a good old-fashioned stakeout.

It was a boring three hours before anything happened, but at around 8pm, she emerged from the flat with Sam, all dressed up for a night out.

I had seen her a million times in my mind, but it was the first time I had seen her in the flesh. She was everything I imagined, and I had to resist a strong urge to run up to her and fling my arms around her there and then.

I had waited this long. Two more weeks wouldn't make much difference. Her being here, at the flat, was very promising, but it wasn't enough. I needed to know for sure that she was still bound for San Antonio.

I gave them a minute to get clear then got out of the car and began following them down the street, about a hundred yards behind. I knew what I was doing was akin to stalking, but I would be fine provided they didn't spot me.

After about a mile, they went into a pub on the outskirts of town. I followed them in, discreetly, and took up a position at the other end of the bar, far away from them, as they ordered their drinks.

It was lively in the pub, but not packed. A DJ was setting up, but he didn't look like he would be starting for a while. Once I had my drink I went and sat at a table close enough to them to eavesdrop. I made sure I sat with my back to them because I couldn't risk Sarah seeing my face.

Within five minutes I had heard all I needed to know as they chatted away excitedly in their Welsh accents. All the talk was of their forthcoming holiday which meant everything was going according to plan. Taking care not to be seen, I surreptitiously slipped out of the pub. I could return to Oxford with my mind at ease.

Nick & I flew out to Ibiza a week before Sarah & Sam and spent the week 'having it large' in Manumission, Es Paradis, and Café Del Mar. I was relaxed, happy and full of anticipation for what lay ahead.

I did not doubt that she would be where she should be, exactly as I had pictured it so many times. On the night in question, a pub crawl had been arranged for all the new arrivals on the holiday. Everyone was to meet up in the bar of the hotel in which we were staying.

It was there that we would see Sarah and Sam for the first time, though we wouldn't approach them until we reached another bar, later in the pub crawl. I knew the precise place and time and exactly what to say. The scene had been replayed in my dreams a thousand times.

Since returning from Swansea, I hadn't had a moment's concern that anything might go wrong. So, when we went down to the bar and she wasn't where I expected her to be, I had a moment of mild panic. I looked around desperately but couldn't see either of them. Then I started asking other people if they had seen her.

It was all to no avail.

She wasn't there.

Chapter Twelve - Sarah

Gareth was a waste of space and I'd had enough.

Many people at the end of relationships say things like "I don't know what I ever saw in him," but that wasn't true in my case. We were both twenty when we met, back in the early 1990s. I was working as a trainee legal secretary, him as a mechanic at a garage close to my home in Swansea.

He was fit, fun, and he made me laugh. He loved his cars and couldn't get enough of them. Outside of work, he bought vintage cars and did them up. On our very first date he picked me up in a red, open-topped MG Midget he had rescued from a scrap yard and restored to almost mint condition.

Most of our fun revolved around drinking. Pubs, parties, nightclubs, you name it, it was going on nearly every night. We were both still living with our parents and had plenty of disposable income. We were full of energy at that age, quite happily clubbing until 2am. Then we'd roll home, stopping off somewhere for a little naughty fun on the way, before presenting at work, fresh as a daisy, at 9am the next morning.

There wasn't a lot of romance, but the physical side more than made up for that. They were exciting times, but the party had to end sometime, which it did not long after we got a flat together.

We had envisaged having more fun than ever now we had our own place. It would be sex on tap, as he described it.

But the reality was somewhat different. Now we were living together, the thrill had gone. The endless partying was also becoming tiring. We were in our mid-twenties by now, and I was keen to settle down, but Gareth wasn't. He just wanted to carry on boozing and was hardly ever at home.

Our flat was tiny with no outside space, so when he wasn't at work or the pub, he was round at his parents' place. He would spend all weekend round there, doing up another of his old cars in their garage. I saw less of him than before we were living together.

Then he got done for drink-driving. Ironically, this was something he was fiercely opposed to. He had proudly declared on many an occasion that he would never get behind the wheel after a drink. Unfortunately, he hadn't considered the morning after factor.

It was all very well sinking eight pints and walking home from the pub, but what happened when you got up seven hours later to drive to work? He had always dismissed this, saying he had slept it off, but it was still in his system and one morning his luck ran out. A car pulled out of a T-junction right in front of him and he couldn't avoid a collision.

The other driver was clearly at fault, but that didn't help Gareth. No-one was hurt but the accident blocked the road, the police were called, and both drivers breathalysed. Only Gareth was over the limit. A £1000 fine and a twelve-month ban from driving swiftly followed.

He was dealt a further blow shortly afterwards when the garage where he worked announced they were laying off staff. Without a driving licence, he was the first to get the chop, and getting another job in the industry was impossible. The country was still suffering the aftermath of a lengthy recession and few were hiring – especially not convicted drink-drivers.

When I suggested tentatively that he might want to learn from this and cut down on the alcohol, he reacted angrily, telling me I had no right to tell him what he could or couldn't do. I encouraged him to look for a job outside the motor trade, but he wasn't interested. Instead, he spent all day sitting around the flat drinking and playing racing games on his bloody Nintendo. Meanwhile, I went to work to pay for it all.

He got increasingly moody and belligerent, but I rode it out, telling myself it was only for a year. After that, he would get his licence back, get a new job and get his act together. That should have happened in summer 1997, but there was to be no triumphant return to work when his ban was served. He had become used to his layabout lifestyle and simply couldn't be arsed.

One afternoon, I came home and found him asleep on the floor, surrounded by empty cans, and with a prominent stain on his trouser crotch where he had wet himself. I decided to follow the advice my best friend Sam had given me, and moved out that night, into the spare room in her flat.

Sam was single. Free from the constraints of relationships, we embraced the concept of girl power, as promoted by the hugely successful Spice Girls. After a memorable weekend at the Reading Festival in 1997, Sam suggested we upped our game the following summer and signed us up for a Club 18-30 holiday.

I was under no illusions about what went on during those holidays but had no reservations about embracing it. The ladette culture was in full swing and we could behave just like the lads, without being labelled slags as would have been the case in the past.

We travelled light, skimpy tops, shorts, and swimsuits. Our flight at Gatwick was delayed for two hours which gave us plenty of time to hit the shops. There had been a recent story in the news that duty-free was soon to be abolished within the EU. We made sure we took full advantage of our allocation while we could; a bottle of Smirnoff for me and Bacardi Spice for Sam.

Once we'd emerged from the shop, stuffing our bottles into our hand luggage, we headed for Boots where we both picked up a 12 pack of condoms and some factor 25 sun cream. It was best to be prepared on all fronts, Sam had said.

I wondered if factor 25 would be high enough for me. I was fair, with pale skin that burnt easily. Sam was darker, with a more olive skin tone. She was more concerned whether 12 condoms would be enough and was debating if she should buy two packs. That seemed optimistic, even considering the type of holiday we were going on.

We were on a standard, package holiday flight in cattle class to Ibiza. It was one of those Boeing planes with a single aisle down the centre and three rather small seats on either side. We were packed in like the proverbial sardines.

The plane was full of young people like us, eagerly chatting away, full of nervous excitement about the experiences that lay ahead. For us, the adventure was to start before we left the airport when there was an unexpected development.

We had an interminable wait at the baggage carousel, where for a good half an hour the only item circulating was a battered old khaki suitcase. Ignored by all, it looked as if it had been going around forever. Eventually, our luggage arrived, and we headed for the exit, keen to find our way to the coach that would take us down into San Antonio.

As soon as we exited into the foyer, it was clear something was going on. There was an excited crowd gathering at the end of the hall, where the Club 18-30 reps were waiting to greet the holidaymakers. Something was attracting their attention, but it was difficult to see what it was from this distance.

"What's all that about?" asked Sam.

"I don't know, but the reps are over there, so let's go and find out."

As we approached the excited gaggle, who seemed to be mostly women, a familiar figure emerged from the crowd, walking straight towards us. It wasn't someone we knew personally, but we had seen him on TV hundreds of times.

"Oh my God!" exclaimed Sam. "It's Ben Lewis. And he's coming over here!"

Nearly everyone in Britain must have known who Ben Lewis was. He was a huge star of film and TV, having just starred in a major action movie, not to mention his award-winning sitcom. Some were talking about him as a possible future James Bond.

He was also incredibly rich, rumoured to be a billionaire, all self-made. What was he doing here in Ibiza? And most importantly, what did he want with us? As he approached, it was clear he wasn't just randomly walking in our direction. He was making a beeline directly for us.

As he reached us, he broke into a huge grin and uttered his famous catchphrase, "How's it going?"

I was almost speechless. One of the most famous people on the planet was talking to me. I was tongue-tied, unsure of what to say.

"I'm good, thank you, Mr Lewis," I managed to say, somehow without stammering, before adding, "Can I have your autograph?"

I couldn't believe I had come out with such a boring and predictable question. He probably heard that dozens of times a day. This is what happens when you are put on the spot in an overawing situation and say the first thing that comes into your head.

"Please, call me Ben," he said. "And you are?"

"Sarah," I replied. "And this is Sam."

"Well, Sarah," he said, "I'm staying in the best villa on the island for a few days. Want to come and check it out?"

I couldn't believe it. Ben Lewis wanted me to come to his villa! Me! A nobody from Swansea! I was completely bowled over.

He was full of warmth and charm. How could I possibly refuse?

"Well, we are meant to be getting a coach to our hotel," I said. "But I guess we could."

"Oh, no offence to your friend here," he said, passing a cursory glance in Sam's direction. "But I did mean just you."

I saw Sam's face fall, and a moment of doubt about all this came to mind. Why didn't he want her to come too?

I quickly came to a decision. I might be risking missing out on the ultimate claim to fame moment, but I wasn't about to ditch my best friend, the one who had taken me in after things had fallen apart with Gareth.

"Sorry," I said. "But we come as a package. It's both of us or not at all."

I saw a brief flicker of annoyance cross his face, but then he beamed his big smile again.

"Of course, she can come," he said. "The more the merrier. Wait till you see the sunset from the villa across the bay. It's amazing."

"What about our hotel?" asked Sam. "We do have to check-in."

"Oh, don't worry about that," said Ben. "I'll get my chauffeur to run you down there later. Speaking of which, my limo's outside. Shall we?"

"Why not," I said, scarcely believing this was happening.

We emerged from the front door of the airport into the baking July sun, blazing down from a clear blue sky. Ben was as good as his word, his limo parked directly in front of the doors, framed by the rows of palm trees in the background.

A handsome, young chauffeur, dressed in suit and hat, took our cases, put them in the boot, then held open the door for us. He must have been baking in all that gear in this heat. Surprisingly, there were very few people outside. I had been expecting to find a crowd of photographers waiting for someone like Ben, but it was surprisingly quiet.

"No paparazzi?" I enquired, as we climbed into the limo, Ben following behind us. The chauffeur firmly closed the door, shutting out the disappointed gaggle of women who had followed us out of the airport.

"They don't know I'm here yet," replied Ben. "One of the advantages of having a private jet. And the internet is still in its infancy."

"The internet?" asked Sam. "That's just a fad, isn't it?"

"Oh, it's way more than that," replied Ben. "Give it a few years and you won't be able to do anything without someone filming it and posting it online."

He reached over and opened a fridge door in the spacious rear compartment in which we were now seated. I had never been in a limo before and was amazed at how much room there was.

"Champagne, anyone?" he inquired, pulling out an expensive bottle. "This is an excellent vintage – Dom Pérignon, 1990."

He pressed a button beside the fridge, and a hatch opened. A tray slid out smoothly, rather like a compact disc player, with four glasses on it.

"Classy," said Sam, clearly impressed.

"Mind yourselves," he said, as he eased the cork out of the bottle. "These things can be a bit unpredictable in a confined space."

The cork hit the roof with tremendous force and ricocheted around the car but didn't hit anyone. He quickly poured the drinks, handing them to each of us in turn.

"To new friends!" he said, raising his glass and clinking it with ours. "Cheers!"

I sipped my champagne, and looked out of the window, at the dusty, sandy landscape passing by outside. The car was climbing uphill, away from the coast, passing abandoned, unfinished buildings. I needed to try and come up with something interesting to say to make up for my earlier, lame autograph request. But I couldn't think of anything other than small talk.

"What brings you to Ibiza, Ben?" was the best I could come up with.

"Oh, I'm just taking a little break from filming," he said. "I fancied a holiday and keep hearing about the great club scene here, so I thought I'd come out and give it a try."

"Do you invite every girl you meet back to your villa?" asked Sam, who had a more suspicious nature than me. She wouldn't have forgotten that Ben hadn't wanted to bring her.

"Only the special ones," he replied, making eye contact with me, and holding my gaze.

I felt weak at the knees. This was quite surreal. I was sitting in a limo, sipping champagne, with one of the most famous film stars on the planet.

The car passed through some black, metal gates and glided smoothly up a tarmac drive to stop in front of a magnificent looking villa.

"We're here," he announced, as the driver opened the door to let us out. "Welcome to my humble abode."

"Hardly humble," replied Sam, as we marvelled at the beautiful, whitewashed building. There were some impressive houses back home in the Langland Bay area, but nothing quite on this scale.

The roof was red slate, and it had turrets on each corner. The surrounding gardens were immaculate, with not a blade of grass out of place.

"It looks more like a castle than a villa," I remarked.

"It's got eight bedrooms and six bathrooms," boasted Ben. "Oh, and a swimming pool, sauna and jacuzzi. Come and have a look around."

The interior was just as impressive as the outside. It reeked of wealth, all marble floors and pillars and was immaculately clean. The kitchen was huge and futuristic, with every mod con you could imagine. This included the biggest and most impressive looking coffee machine I had ever seen. It was like something out of *Star Trek*.

"Do you own this place?" I asked.

"It belongs to one of France's top footballers," he replied. "He's away at the World Cup at the moment and said I could have it for a few weeks."

We walked through the kitchen and out onto the terrace beyond, where there was a sizeable, landscaped swimming pool. There was a balcony on the far side, with a stunning view beyond across the Mediterranean. He hadn't been exaggerating when he had said it was the best view in Ibiza.

"My chauffeur has put your cases in the hall," said Ben. "I'm guessing you brought your swimsuits. Pick a bedroom, any you like, and get changed. I'll see you out by the pool."

We made our way up the marble, curving staircase that dominated the front hall, and picked a random bedroom. It was as luxurious and spacious as every other room in the house. There was no sign of any staff, but there had to be plenty of people employed to keep the place in such a pristine condition.

"I can't believe this is happening," I said as I eased my sweaty underwear off. This was a huge relief after so many hours in hot airports and the cramped conditions on the plane.

"Are you sure this is a good idea?" asked Sam.

"How do you mean?" I replied, curious as to why she had reservations.

"To begin with, don't you think it's a little odd how he made a beeline straight for you at the airport?" she asked. "It's almost as if he was expecting you. And why you, in particular?" she asked, casting her eye over my naked body.

"Do you mind not eyeing me up?" I objected.

"Don't get me wrong, you've got a pretty decent figure, but you're no supermodel. So why is he so interested in you?"

"I did wonder that myself," I replied, "but what does it matter? We're getting to hang out with an A-lister at his luxury villa. Let's just go with the flow."

"OK, but I'm still a little nervous. You must have heard the rumours about him. They were splashed all over the tabloids last weekend."

"You know I don't read those papers," I replied. "Celebrity gossip and tittle-tattle don't interest me."

"I had better fill you in then. There have been a lot of stories recently about him mistreating women. *The News of the World* last week was full of kiss and tell stories about him from some high-class Hollywood hookers."

"Prostitution isn't illegal," I countered, "even if it is seedy."

"Yeah, but he was stringing these women along, pretending he was going to get them acting roles. He was playing the classic casting couch scenario. As for the legality, that depends on which state you're in. I am fairly sure it's illegal in California."

"I suppose you've got a point," I replied. "Why did you come along then?"

"To protect you, of course. You're my best friend. And there's more than just the hookers to worry about. His girlfriend wasn't seen in public for months and there were rumours he was knocking her about. Her former maid claimed he'd beaten her black and blue and that she'd had to have plastic surgery to repair her nose."

"He seems so charming, though," I said, but I was a little concerned. I trusted Sam's instincts. They had always been reliable in the past.

"Most snakes are until they bite you. Just be careful."

"I'm sure I'll be perfectly safe," I replied. "I've got you here to protect me, for a start."

"You do, but he wasn't too keen on me coming along, was he? What if I wasn't here? Come to that, does it not worry you that absolutely no-one knows we're here? We didn't even check in with the rep at the airport. As far as Club 18-30 are concerned, we never arrived. They might even have given our room at the hotel to someone else by now."

"You're worrying unnecessarily," I said, trying to convince myself. "Everything's going to be fine."

I really hoped I was right.

Chapter Thirteen - Ben

Wow, I was getting good at this! Even by my standards, I had surpassed myself this time.

The last decade had been one non-stop party. What a difference knowledge of future events had made! In my first few weeks in 1988, I had barely begun to contemplate how much I could achieve.

In the early days, it was all about placing accumulative bets on sporting events I knew the result of in advance. But there were limits. Even the biggest bookmakers in Britain had a maximum pay-out of a million pounds. After I had hit that a couple of times, I found future bets being politely declined.

No matter, I had put a couple of million away and that was enough for me to move into where the real money was – the stock market.

At the start of the 1990s, hardly anyone had a mobile phone, or a computer at home. And virtually nobody had heard of the internet. Over the next decade that would change beyond all recognition and I would be in from the start, investing in IT, software, and telecoms.

It was incredibly easy. I was shrewd enough to get into some start-up companies that I knew would be household names by the end of the century. By 1998, my millions had turned into billions.

If you've got it, flaunt it, they say, and boy, did I flaunt it! Fast cars, watches, expensive suits – I had it all and showed them off at every opportunity. I loved seeing the looks of jealousy on poor people's faces when I cruised by in my latest acquisition.

They were peasants, the lot of them, and I despised them. But peasants were necessary and had been since the early days of feudalism. I needed people like them to do all the hard work so that people like me could live in luxury. They earned bugger all but still gave a chunk of it back to the treasury in taxes. I wasn't that stupid and set myself up in the tax haven of Monaco.

I wasn't that bothered about Thomas and Charlotte anymore. They were irrelevant, but I couldn't resist going back to college one last time to rub their noses in it. I couldn't have scripted a more delightful exchange if I had tried, especially when I found out he had got her pregnant. It was the sweetest icing on the cake I could have hoped for. Game set and match to me.

Even discovering that one of them, probably her, had keyed my new Ferrari in a pique of spite didn't bother me. It just showed I had got to them. One quick paint job later, and I was good to go again.

Within a year of that, I started jet setting, in club class. I wanted to rub shoulders with the rich and famous. Monte Carlo was a good place to start, where I hung out with Grand Prix drivers in casinos. That was great, but the place where I could really make my name was Hollywood.

It was remarkable how easy it was to integrate my way into that community. Money opens doors, and if you had it, you could be one of them. Some might think that vulgar, but I call it human nature. People like to hang out with people who are like them, and nowhere is that more apparent than in L.A.

I rented a fantastic house in a gated community full of actors, producers, and various other Hollywood bigwigs. The rent was something ludicrous in the region of $50,000 a month, but it was worth every cent to validate me as a bona fide member of the community.

I went out of my way to get to know my neighbours, calling on them to offer friendship and welcome gifts of food and drink, flown in from Europe. They seemed fascinated by my English accent, which I exaggerated, doing a passable impression of Hugh Grant. It was easy to rip him off as *Four Weddings and a Funeral* was still a few years away and no-one in America had heard of him yet.

They lapped it up and before long I was being invited to all sorts of events and parties. I was well and truly part of the in-crowd.

When people asked what I did for a living, I claimed to be an actor, and that most of the work I had done was back in the UK. Most seemed to accept this, but if they pressed further for evidence of my credentials, I explained I had mainly worked in theatre. That was why they hadn't seen me in any films or TV shows. This was long before the days of IMDb and Wikipedia, so it was hard for anyone to fact check up on me.

I wasn't sure if I could act or not, but I was doing a rather good job of pretending to be someone I wasn't. The idea of being an actor appealed to me. It was all very well making billions on the stock market, but I wanted more than just money. I wanted fame.

Being young, twenty and rich gave me access to some of the most beautiful women in the world and I spent several months shagging my way around California. The accent helped too – the birds over there loved it. I had no desire to acquire a girlfriend, not when I could have whoever I wanted.

However, when I met up-and-coming actress, Cindy, that all changed. Her father was one of the most famous directors in town. This was why she was getting so many acting roles because she couldn't act for toffee.

She couldn't do anything, to be honest. She had been spoiled since birth on Daddy's money and had made no effort at school whatsoever. She had grown up to be little more than a dumb blonde with an annoying laugh and ridiculously large fake breasts. She had spent a fortune on them as soon as she came of age and got access to her trust funds.

I couldn't stand her, but that was irrelevant. She was my potential ticket to the big time, so I showered her with tacky jewellery, flowers, and other gifts. This was all part of my plan to delude her into thinking I loved her, which wasn't difficult with someone with an IQ as low as hers. Once I had ensnared her, I planned to use her to further my acting career until I didn't need her anymore. Then I would cast her aside.

I couldn't be seen to be messing around with other women behind her back so developed a taste for high-class Hollywood hookers. These fulfilled my ever-increasing sexual desires behind Cindy's back and were very discreet. These women kissed, but never told, which is bloody well how it ought to be with the amount of money I was paying them.

In the spring of 1990, I got a call from my old pal, Julian, inviting me to his posh society wedding. This was being held back home at some pretentious Oxford college. I jumped at the chance. It would be an opportunity to show just how far I had come compared to them.

I took Cindy along for good measure, with strict instructions to keep her mouth shut as much as possible. I wanted her merely as a trinket to drape on my arm because not being the brightest tool in the box, she might embarrass me.

What I hadn't expected was running into Thomas. I had barely thought about him for a couple of years, but here he was again. This time he gave me some tall story about a mysterious time-travelling man he wanted me to go and meet. He was under the misguided impression I would welcome the chance to return to my own time and I quickly put him straight on that front.

Not for the first time, I felt great irritation towards Thomas. Ever since I had arrived in 1988, he had been trying to interfere in my life. He always took the moral high ground, and I knew he considered himself superior to me, even though I was way richer than him. I'd had enough and decided I needed to get my own back.

What would hurt him the most? After I returned to L.A. I mulled it over one night with a couple of bottles of vintage wine. Then I had a flash of inspiration. I knew exactly what I needed to do. I had the means to ruin his life. The only drawback was that I was going to have to wait a few years to put my plan into action, but it would be worth the wait.

In the meantime, it wasn't just my tech stocks that were soaring in value. My personal stock value in Hollywood was rocketing too. Cindy was becoming an utter pain in the arse, but I kept up the pretence, particularly around her father to whom I sucked up at every possible opportunity. This involved learning to play golf, a game which I had always thought a complete waste of time.

He loved it though, so I made the effort to further ingratiate myself. That meant spending many an hour listening to the boring crap that he and his golfing pals spouted on the course, but I felt it was worth the investment. One time, I even got to meet Donald Trump, and jokingly suggested to him that he should run for president one day. He laughed and said, "Stranger things have happened."

When I suggested to Cindy's father that I might be about to propose to her, my first supporting film role swiftly followed. My big break came a couple of years after that when he recommended me to an executive at NBC who was casting for a major new sitcom.

It was a huge hit, and suddenly I was a star. Everywhere I went, women wanted not just my autograph, but my body too. There was only one slight problem with this. I was by now married to Cindy.

Now my acting career was established, she was becoming surplus to requirements. She was becoming whinier and more annoying than ever, always wanting me to go places and do stuff with her. All I wanted to do was go out, party, and bang some starry-eyed fan. Which is pretty much what I did most of the time.

It didn't take long for the press to pick up on my extracurricular activities. They had developed the unwelcome habit of following me about and I didn't like it. When Cindy confronted me about my infidelity, she started screaming hysterically at me and trying to beat me, pummelling me with her arms.

When I took hold of her to try and restrain her, she claimed I was hurting her and a couple of days later was showing me the bruises on her arm. She claimed I had done it and that she was going to show her father. I suspect that she inflicted them herself because it was not like I had grabbed her that hard, but I knew no-one would believe me.

I did my best to pacify her, promising her I'd change my ways and a load of other bullshit I had no intention of following. It was only for a few weeks until all evidence of the bruises had gone, then I could ditch her. It wouldn't be that big a deal. Hollywood must have had one of the highest divorce rates in the world. It would have been more unusual if our marriage had lasted.

This all happened in the spring of 1998, which was the year when Thomas was going to get a great big dish of revenge, served suitably cold.

It had been eight years since I had last seen him, but I'm sure he was aware of what I had been doing. He could not possibly have missed my rise to fame, and it amused me to think of him getting more and more exasperated about it.

That wasn't nearly enough. I wanted far more. I wanted to do something that would devastate him and cause him to feel utter despair, the sort that drives a man to take his own life. The best moment would be when he came to realise, he had been the author of his own demise.

Right from the moment I first arrived in 1988, he had been banging on about his precious Sarah and how nothing must prevent them from fulfilling their star-crossed destiny. What a load of soppy, romantic twaddle! He should have kept his mouth shut.

He had given me enough details during one of our conversations to hang himself with. I knew that Sarah was from Swansea, and would be travelling to Ibiza with her friend, Sam, in July 1988. That was all the information I needed.

The rest I found out using private detectives who were able to find out exactly when both Sarah and Thomas were travelling to Ibiza. I had an ex-CIA hacker on my payroll who could get into anything. If there was something I needed to know, he would find it.

He did this by hacking into various systems to track holiday bookings and passenger lists. Thomas was easy to track as I knew his full name.

Sarah was a little more difficult as I did not know her surname and there were many people named Sarah – it was a common name. However, there was only one flying to Ibiza at the right time who ticked all the boxes. She lived in Swansea, had booked with another girl called Samantha, and was the right age. Her flight from Cardiff was exactly a week after Thomas was due to fly out.

As luck would have it, one of my footballer friends in Monaco had a luxury villa in Ibiza he wouldn't be using in the summer. He was happy to let me have it for a few weeks. I arrived a few days before Sarah was due, to ensure everything was in place.

I was cutting things a little fine, but any earlier and I risked being spotted and hounded by the paparazzi. I didn't want Thomas to find out I was there, because he might twig what I was up to. I needed to keep a low profile. A cockney bloke from a neighbouring villa attempted to strike up a conversation with me one day, but I told him where to go and he didn't bother me again.

Things had gone distinctly pear-shaped back in L.A. and Cindy was again threatening to blow the whistle, citing cruelty and violence against me. It was hardly violence, in my opinion. She had started bleating on at me about our relationship right in the middle of a NASCAR race. She was standing in front of the TV, so I told her to move and shut up.

She wouldn't so I hurled an empty beer bottle at her. It didn't even hit her, but she still went bloody apeshit, accusing me of domestic violence and threatening to go to the papers. That was it, I was out of there.

I told her I had business in Europe and flew over to Monaco for a couple of days, before flying on to Ibiza. I was so rich now that I had my own private jet and getting on to the island undetected was easy. I could remain incognito until the day Sarah arrived.

I knew when she would arrive, down to the minute. On the day I had intelligence on the ground to tell me when her luggage was being loaded on to the carousel. This seemed to take forever due to the shocking inefficiency of the local baggage handlers. It reminded me how glad I was that in my new life I no longer had to fly on those frightful airlines!

Once I got the green light that she was almost through, it was a simple case of emerging into the arrivals area and waiting. I had photographs of her from every angle which had been taken by my private detective. There would be no mistaking her.

The only hindrance would be the inevitable gaggle of women who would be fawning all over me as soon as they saw me. This lot had all flown in from Wales where they had a habit of throwing their knickers at Tom Jones. They would probably be even worse than the American fans I usually had to deal with.

Everything went according to plan. I politely weathered the storm of the adoring fans, signed a few autographs, then made my way through the hall, directed by a couple of men I had tracking Sarah and Sam. From there it was just a case of using my considerable charm to whisk them away in my limo to my secluded villa, far away from prying eyes.

I had only been in the airport for about ten minutes, so there hadn't been time for the press to get wind of my presence. My chauffeur made good speed and I was confident that we hadn't been followed. I was very keen that we would not be disturbed.

I had hired several local peasants to scrub the villa from top to toe that morning. The pool and gardens were pristine, there was not a speck of dust anywhere inside, and the fridge and bar were stocked with everything we could ever need.

I had found that the Spanish workers did a grand job if you greased their palms with enough pesetas. They were under strict instructions to vacate the villa by siesta time and not to return until the evening of the following day. Everything was set up to perfection.

My one disappointment was that I couldn't be in San Antonio to witness Thomas's distress when his beloved Sarah failed to show up. That moment would be crushing and soul-destroying and I would have savoured the moment if I had been there. No matter, I couldn't be everywhere, and I would enjoy revealing the truth to him in due course.

All I had to do now was seduce Sarah. This had been my plan all along. It would be the ultimate victory for me over Thomas, hopefully, one he would never get over. If I'm being honest, I didn't fancy her much. She was mildly pretty, in a girl next door sort of way, but I was used to banging the most beautiful women in the world. I also found her Welsh accent irritating.

But this wasn't about her looks. Nailing her was worth a hundred supermodels to get one over on Thomas. The beauty of my plan was that she was completely oblivious to what was going on.

She had no idea of what should have happened today if I hadn't intervened. A big movie, *Sliding Doors*, had recently come out about a woman following two different timelines. She may well have seen it. Little did she know, she was now starring in her real-life version. And it was all down to me.

Now we were back at the villa, it would be easy. After all, who wouldn't want to shag me? Who wouldn't want to shag a famous film star? Most people, I believe. They get starstruck and it doesn't matter if they are in a relationship.

You wouldn't believe how many married women have dropped their knickers for me then gone dutifully home to their husbands, who were none the wiser. I'd done them a favour and spiced up their life. They would also have a claim to fame they could boast to their closest girl pals about.

The only stumbling block with Sarah was her ugly friend, Sam. At least I wouldn't have to do her too unless they insisted on a threesome, of which I had previously had plenty.

She was being a killjoy all night, constantly reminding Sarah that they needed to get to their accommodation. I just kept the champagne flowing, charming Sarah with my tales of life in Hollywood and hoping Sam would loosen up with a few drinks inside her. She wouldn't let it drop, though.

"I really think we ought to get back to the resort, Sarah," she said for the umpteenth time, as I poured more champagne into my quarry's glass. We were sitting out on the wicker furniture on the patio by the pool, overlooking the bay. Night had long since fallen, but the sky was lit up by the distant lights across the bay. We were about four miles from San Antonio.

I sat back down on the yellow seat covers, inching ever closer to Sarah.

"Chill out," I said to Sam. "Why don't you two stay here tonight? It's late now and we've all had plenty to drink. You can check-in at your hotel tomorrow, no problem."

"That's if our rooms are still there," said Sam. "They've probably given them to somebody else by now."

"Oh, I guarantee you'll get in," I replied. "I'll come to the hotel and personally ensure it. You don't have to throw much of this stuff at the locals around here to get what you want."

I pulled a wad of 5,000 peseta notes out of my wallet and waved them in Sam's direction.

"Besides, you want to stay, don't you babe," I asked, turning to Sarah. She looked at me, and I leaned in for the kiss, to which she readily acceded.

I'd done it! She was mine for the taking.

"I do," replied Sarah, breaking out of the kiss.

"You can go if you want, Sam," I said. "I'll call my chauffeur and get him to take you. Sarah won't mind, will you?"

"I'm not leaving her here with you," retorted Sam. "I know what sort of a man you are."

"That doesn't sound very friendly," I said. "Not after I have been so accommodating."

"Does your wife know what you get up to?" she asked.

"You don't want to believe everything you read in the papers, darling," I replied.

It was a struggle to keep up my charming, smiling persona because I was bristling inside at Sam's attitude. I was used to women worshipping the ground I walked on and this one wasn't playing ball.

"Sarah, you're not seriously going to have sex with him, are you?" she asked.

Sarah looked back at her friend and just gave a sheepish smile.

"Oh, you are," said Sam. "Well spare me from witnessing any more. I'm tired after the flight and I'm off to bed. You do what you feel best, but I think you'll regret it in the morning. Speaking of which, we're out of here first thing, right?"

"Of course," said Sarah. "Sleep tight."

"Don't be noisy," said Sam, as she got up from her chair, and headed back inside.

Result! With Sam out of the way, there was nothing to stop me.

"Fancy a spot of skinny-dipping?" I asked.

She grinned and peeled off her bikini top, revealing a perky pair of breasts. This was just getting better and better. She was well up for it. Was this the saintly Sarah that Thomas had described?

"Come on," she said, peeling off her bottom half and leaping into the pool. I needed no second invitation, and we were soon frolicking and splashing around. I couldn't give a toss whether Sam heard or not. I'd make as much noise as I damn well-liked.

In the pool, we indulged in what I had often seen bossy notices around swimming pools refer to as heavy petting. From there, it was an easy progression to take her back to my room, where I was to do the dirty deed.

As our coupling reached its inevitable conclusion, I was filled with an immense sense of satisfaction, as if I had just scored the winning goal for England in the World Cup Final. It wasn't the best sex I'd ever had, far from it, but it was the most triumphant.

What made it all the sweeter was that in the heat of the moment, she hadn't said anything about wearing a condom, and I certainly wasn't going to suggest it. It amused me no end to think she might become pregnant. Wouldn't that be one in the eye for Thomas, after what he'd done to Charlotte?

Afterwards, she wanted to be all lovey-dovey and snuggle up to me. I hate it when women do that, but I went along with it until she fell asleep, then I went back out to the poolside. I poured myself a large single malt, and revelled in the glory of my conquest, catching occasional far-off snippets of rave music on the breeze. There was an outdoor club a couple of miles away which went on all night.

What now? Seek out Thomas, with Sarah in tow, and gloat? It was tempting, but what if it didn't work out as I hoped. What if they truly were destined for each other and fell in love at first sight? I don't believe in all that romantic nonsense, whatever the movies like to portray. I have never fallen in love with anyone and I'm glad about it.

He wouldn't want her now, would he? She was soiled goods and not just by some random Welshman from the rough end of Swansea, but by me – his nemesis. Once I had rubbed his nose in it, he might never be able to look at her the same way again.

But I couldn't be sure about that. Knowing him, he was probably one of these understanding types who would forgive her, since she couldn't possibly have known what was going on. More fool him, but it might be prudent to keep them apart a little longer. He was bound to be in San Antonio, looking for her. For now, the villa was the best place for her.

I would get her to stay a while longer which would also give me more opportunities to try and get her pregnant. The more I thought about it, the more I was developing a burning desire to plant my own seed within her. If I did that, Thomas would never accept her.

Of course, I had no intention of bringing up a child with her or indeed having any sort of relationship. I was already bored with her, but I just needed to put up with her for a couple more days. The longer I kept her and Thomas apart, the better. He had told me she had got pregnant very soon after they had met, possibly even on this holiday.

If that were true, she'd be fertile right now which would give me an even greater chance to hit the target. Even if she did eventually end up with him and get pregnant, there was no guarantee that the baby would be his. He would have nine months of worrying about it, not knowing if it was mine or his.

The thought of how devastated he would be if the baby did turn out to be mine filled me with glee! Even by my standards, this was a fiendishly evil plan, and I was thoroughly enjoying carrying it out.

The following morning, I got up early and contacted the housekeeper, gardener, and pool guy, to tell them all to take the day off. I didn't want any witnesses to what I might have to do. Then I went and woke Sarah up, taking the opportunity to get frisky with her again, an activity in which she was all too eager to participate. The more shots I put on target, the greater the chance of hitting the back of the net.

By the time we made our way back through to the kitchen, in matching silk dressing gowns that I'd picked up on a trip to Japan, Sam was waiting for us. She was pottering about in the kitchen, making breakfast out of fruit and some yoghurt she had found in the fridge.

"I thought I told you two to be quiet," she snapped.

"Oh, I'm sorry, I didn't realise this was your villa," I replied sarcastically. "Help yourself, by the way," I added, in the same tone.

"And put some proper clothes on, Sarah," she added. "You look bloody ridiculous. What are you now, some sort of geisha girl?"

"Come on, Sam, don't be like that," said Sarah. "We're on holiday."

"And it's about time we got started on that holiday," she replied. "As soon as we've had breakfast, we need to get to our hotel. If it's not too much trouble, Ben, could you call your chauffeur, please?"

"There's no need to rush off," I said, determined not to let them leave. "Why don't you stay another day? I've got a luxury yacht in the harbour. How about a tour around the island?"

I looked across at Sarah, but she looked a little hesitant. She cast her eyes back and forth between the two of us, her loyalties divided.

"I don't know, maybe we ought to go and check-in at the hotel first."

"Oh, stop worrying about that, I said I'd sort it, didn't I?"

"That's all very well," said Sam, "but we didn't come here to spend all week with you, no matter how rich or famous you are. This is supposed to be a girl power holiday! We want to get drunk, pop a few pills and dance all night. Yes, I know you're a big celeb and all that, and we are grateful for your hospitality, but we have to go now."

"But I insist," I said. "Just one more day, what harm can it do?"

"I'm not staying here a moment longer, and neither are you, are you Sarah?"

"Sorry, Ben, but Sam's right," said Sarah. "I'm here with her and it's been fun, but we need to get going now."

"Not yet," I insisted, feeling increasingly annoyed. I wasn't used to people not doing what I wanted. If they refused to cooperate, I would have to put pressure on them until they did.

"You'll stay here until I say you can go," I added.

"You mean you're keeping us here against our will? I don't think so," snapped Sam. "Come on Sarah, we're leaving right now."

She made her way out of the kitchen towards the front door but when she turned the handle, it wouldn't open.

"Don't bother," I said. "It's locked."

"Ben, what are you doing?" asked Sarah. "Come on, we've had a good time – don't spoil it now."

"You can't leave," I insisted. "I can't let you go into San Antonio."

"You see?" said Sam, triumphantly. "I warned you about him. The rumours are true. He's a control freak, he beats up his wife, goodness knows what else he gets up to. These people with money think they can get away with anything. We should never have come here."

She stormed back down the hall, through the kitchen and out towards the conservatory area that led out to the pool. But she found those doors locked too.

"What the fuck do you think you're playing at?" she shouted at me. "You're going to be in serious trouble if you don't let us leave, I can tell you. What do you think the local police are going to say about this? Let us out this instant, or we'll be straight on to them."

"She's right, Ben, come on. If you let us go now, we won't say anything to the police," said Sarah.

"Ha, the police!" I exclaimed. "You crack me up! I could pay off every officer on this island if I wanted to."

"Really," said Sam, heading back towards the kitchen. "We'll see about that."

"Stay where you are, you bitch," I hissed, attempting to block her way but she sidestepped me and ran to the far end of the kitchen. She grabbed a gleaming, steel chef's knife, with a black handle, from a knife block next to the sink.

"Now let us go," she said. "I'm not afraid to use this."

I looked closely at her. She was shaking but was it with anger or fear? I didn't think she would use the knife, but I didn't want to take any chances.

"You don't have the guts," I said. "But just in case you do, I see your knife, and I raise you this."

I walked across to a large kitchen dresser, opened the top drawer, and felt around below the tea towels until I found the thing I had stashed there when I arrived.

I pulled out my revolver and pointed it straight at her. That took the wind out of her sails, and the look on her face now was without doubt one of fear.

"Ben, this has gone way too far," said Sarah. "Put that down. What are you doing with a gun?"

"Oh, please," I replied. "I live in America; everyone's got one. I've got several. I go hunting all the time. There's nothing more fun than gunning down a few bears in the forest."

"You are utterly vile!" said Sam. "How did you get it over here? Didn't they stop you at the airport?"

"I'm a billionaire! I've got my own jet. I don't have to go through those scanners at the airport like you commoners. I take a gun wherever I go. You never know when it might come in handy. Right now, being a prime example. Now, I suggest you put that knife back where you got it before I get nervous and trigger happy."

"This is kidnapping," said Sam. "You won't get away with it."

"But I will," I said. "If anything happens who will they believe? I'll just say you're a crazed stalker who broke in here and I was defending myself."

"Just put the gun down," said Sarah. "I'll stay with you if you let Sam go."

"What, so she can go straight to the police? How dumb do you think I am?"

"So, what happens now, then?" asked Sam, as she replaced the knife in the block. "You can't keep us here forever."

I pondered for a moment, but before I could reply, the front doorbell rang. This was an added complication I didn't need.

"Don't even think about calling out!" I said, in a low tone of voice. "Move closer together, so I can keep you both in my sights. And keep quiet!"

I was hoping the caller would go away, but they didn't and started spamming the doorbell repeatedly. Had I been rumbled? I didn't see how I could have been. No-one could know I had these two here.

"Stay where I can see you and keep quiet," I said. "I've got this right here," I said, waving the gun in their direction, before concealing it beneath my dressing gown.

I crept towards the door, all ready to give whoever was still ringing the bell over and over a piece of my mind.

Keeping an eye over my shoulder to check where the girls were, I slowly opened the door.

Chapter Fourteen - Thomas

"She's not here," I said to Nick. "How can she not be here?"

"Who's not here?" he replied. "What are you talking about?"

In my distress, I had broken cover. Nick knew nothing of the real reason why we had come to Ibiza. I had never confided anything to him about my strange journey through life. Experience had taught me that the fewer people knew, the better.

I was devastated at Sarah's non-appearance. I had been convinced that her timeline had stayed on track, despite my unscheduled interactions with Charlotte and Ben. My trip to Swansea had suggested all was proceeding according to plan, so how could things have gone wrong at such a late stage?

"Hey, guys, are you ready to party?" called out our rep, a bubbly, curly-haired blonde named Karen. She had to shout to be heard over the sound of one of the latest club hits which were booming out in the bar.

"Let's go and paint the town red!" she added.

There was a loud cheer from the excited crowd of young people, full of anticipation for the night ahead.

I told myself not to panic. All might not be lost. There were several Club 18-30 hotels in San Antonio, and I knew that we would be meeting up with those staying elsewhere later.

Maybe due to some minor deviation she had ended up staying at one of the other places.

I still hadn't answered Nick's questions, and maybe it was time I did. Today was the day when worrying about the timeline ceased to be an issue. As we all trooped out of the hotel, heading for the centre of San Antonio, I deliberately hung back so the two of us would be at the back of the group.

"We need to talk," I said, earnestly.

"Why so serious?" he asked. "We're supposed to be on holiday."

"It is serious, I'm afraid. You might think I'm crazy, but there's something I need to tell you."

It wasn't the ideal time to be getting all this off my chest, at the back of a crowd of rowdy holidaymakers. The group was now starting to sing a song about beer and shagging, egged on by Karen. We held back a little further so I could be heard, then I told him what I could during the ten-minute walk to the first bar.

"What do you think?" I asked hopefully.

"I think you've had too much of that sangria they were giving out at the pool!" he said. "Do you honestly expect me to believe you can see into the future? If you can, prove it. Give me a demonstration."

"Believe it or not, I already have," I said. "In small ways that didn't disrupt the timeline. Remember when you were so convinced that Mariah Carey was going to be Christmas Number One a few years back? You were going to bet your whole bonus on it? Who was it persuaded you to back East 17 instead?"

"That could just have been a lucky guess," he said. "Tell me something that's going to happen in the next five minutes!"

"It doesn't work like that," I replied. "I can't prove it right now, I just need you to play ball, and help me out. I need to find out what's happened to Sarah."

"What's so special about this Sarah?" asked Nick. "You claim she's the love of your life but hang on a minute – you slept with some Scottish girl last night. What was her name? Cathy wasn't it?"

"I had to do that so as not to disrupt the timeline," I replied.

"How very convenient," said Nick, sarcastically. "OK, I'll help you find this mythical Sarah – if she exists. But don't let it dominate the whole evening. I've been here a week and still not managed to pull. I want to try my luck with one of the new recruits tonight, and I don't intend to waste hours on some wild goose chase."

"Trust me, if we find Sarah, you'll pull tonight. She's got a friend called Sam, and my crystal ball tells me she'll be well up for a roll in the sack with you."

"Why didn't you tell me this before? Come to think about it, how much more have you been holding back from me? Did you know my marriage was going to break up?"

"Not at all," I said. "I only tend to see things that affect me directly."

This was a downright lie. I had known from the start that his brief, whirlwind romance, and the subsequent wedding wouldn't last. It had to, otherwise, he wouldn't have come to Ibiza with me. That's why I had let it all play out without interfering.

"You'd better not be lying to me," he said.

"Look, even if I had known, you were besotted with her when you met. If I had said then, you're making a mistake, and you need to call it off, would you have taken any notice? Of course, you wouldn't."

"I suppose you're right," he conceded. "Not that it matters. I still don't believe all this nonsense you're coming out with."

"Look, just humour me," I said. "I won't stop you trying to pull anyone tonight. You normally do a good enough job of messing things up by yourself. I can't believe you asked that chubby girl last night if she was pregnant. You never ask a woman that!"

"Alright, don't rub it in!" he said. "Just because you've pulled on this holiday and I haven't. I can still make up for lost time. If I don't have any luck with the newcomers, I was thinking of having a crack at Karen. I reckon she would be well up for it."

"You've got no chance there, mate," I replied. "It's an unwritten rule, don't you know? The reps only shag each other. The punters are strictly off-limits. However, speaking of Karen, you've given me an idea. Maybe she can help us."

We were approaching the West End, at the beating heart of San Antonio. This area was a tightly packed group of streets which were heaving with British holidaymakers in search of a good time. Almost every building was a themed bar of some sort or another.

The Ibiza club music scene had never been hotter. The charts back home in the UK were packed with dance hits, which could be heard pouring out of every bar. The flashing neon signs lighting up every establishment were reminiscent of the Las Vegas Strip. It was one of the most vibrant places I had ever been to.

Karen and the other reps led us into a bar where Mousse T's song, *Horny*, was blasting out at a high rate of decibels. Inside was all blue, neon lighting, with a long bar and large dance floor area at the back. It was almost empty when we arrived, but filled up rapidly, as the groups from all the Club 18-30 hotels poured in.

I had sent Nick to the bar to get the drinks so I could scour the incoming hordes for any sign of Sarah, but the more that came in, the more my feeling of despair grew. What had happened to her?

I decided that I would try to speak to Karen, but she was surrounded by other reps and holidaymakers. I inched my way through the crowd and finally managed to get her attention. I had to shout loud to make myself heard over the sound of Run-DMC featuring Jason Nevins, and their massive hit from that summer.

"Hi, I wonder if you can help. I'm trying to find my friend who was meant to be staying at our hotel. Her name's Sarah and she was flying in from Cardiff, but she hasn't arrived."

"I'm sorry, I can't discuss the details of other passengers," shouted back Karen.

"You must be able to tell me something!" I insisted. "It's extremely important I find her. I think something's happened to her."

"Sorry, I can barely hear what you're saying," replied Karen. "Come and see me in the rep's office tomorrow morning. I can't deal with this now, we're meant to be partying!"

She turned away and started jumping up and down to the music, encouraging a group of girls to join in. It was clear I wasn't going to get any more help from her tonight. I made my way back towards the crowded bar to see if I could find Nick.

Then, I overheard a conversation that stopped me dead in my tracks. A group of scantily clad girls were drinking some purple concoction through straws from a goldfish bowl. They were talking about someone I knew all too well in their broad, Essex accents.

"I couldn't believe it. Ben Lewis, right here in Ibiza! And look here, he even autographed my tit!"

She lewdly pulled her top down, to reveal a scrawled signature just above her nipple.

"Excuse me," I interrupted, again fighting to be heard over the music. "Did you say, Ben Lewis? As in the film star?"

"Is there any other Ben Lewis?" replied the girl tipsily. Whatever was in the fishbowl, it certainly packed a punch.

"And you say you've seen him? Here in San Antonio?"

"At the airport," she replied. "I offered to give him one, but he went off with two girls in a limo. Lucky bitches."

"What did they look like, these girls?" I demanded.

"I didn't notice, mate. I was too busy eyeing up him. I wish he'd taken me. I'd have let him do whatever he wanted. My mates back home at the tanning salon in Chelmsford would have been well jell!"

"Was one blonde and slim, the other shorter with dark hair?" I insisted.

"I told ya, mate, I dunno. I ain't given up yet, though. I'm hoping we'll bump into him again. We're going to Manumission later, that's where all the top DJ's hang out. If he's going anywhere, that's where he'll be."

"Thanks," I said, ending the conversation as I could see I wasn't going to get any more sense out of her. Nick had appeared with the beers by now, and something almost too horrible to contemplate was preying on my mind.

I steered him towards the door so we could stand outside where we would at least be able to hear ourselves speak. It was baking hot in the bar too, and I needed fresh air after what I had just been told.

"I think I know what's happened to Sarah," I replied. "I think she's been abducted."

"By whom?" he replied. "Aliens? Perhaps we had better call in Mulder and Scully."

"No – by Ben Lewis!"

"The film star? What's he doing here?"

"I used to know him when we were at college in Oxford. He hates me and would do anything to get one over on me. I think he's got to Sarah before I could."

"How could he know about her?"

"Well, I kind of told him."

"Why would you do that? You never told me about my doomed marriage and I'm your best friend. Why would you confide in him?"

"It was all a long time ago," I replied. "When we first met, in the late eighties, I found out he was a time traveller too.

Unfortunately, he and I had differing views about what we ought to do with our knowledge of the future. Foolishly, I gave him far too much information about my long-term plans – including about Sarah."

"I'll say," said Nick. "He doesn't sound like a particularly nice guy, going by some of the stories in the papers lately."

"That's putting it mildly," I said. "He's cheated his way to the top, using people along the way. He's no more talented than anyone else but he used what he knew about the future to get rich and famous."

"You could have done that too," said Nick.

"I didn't want to," I said. "There was only one thing I wanted, and that was Sarah. Now I think he's taken her."

"Then we've got to find her," said Nick.

"You believe me now, then?" I asked. "What about your plans to pull tonight?"

"Let's be honest, you know I probably won't. Not here, anyway, but you did say if we find Sarah, we find her mate, and you said she fancied me. I do have one condition, though."

"What's that?"

"You can forget about protecting the timeline and give me some proper tips about the future when we get home. Don't worry, I'm not planning to turn into the next Ben Lewis. Just a few pointers to make life a little comfortable – as you did with East 17."

"You've got yourself a deal," I said. "So where shall we start?"

"I thought you'd know. You're the one who can see into the future."

"Not into this," I replied. "I can only see stuff that I experienced in my previous lives. This didn't happen before."

"We've got very little to go on, then," said Nick. "He could be anywhere on the island."

"Well, we're not going to get any answers out of the Club 18-30 crowd," I replied. "Perhaps we ought to try speaking to the locals."

"The Spaniards?" he inquired.

"No, I was thinking more of the ex-pats. There's a strong community of them in all the Spanish resorts and I am sure they will be clued up on what's going on. We need to go and find one of their pubs."

We left the bar, and walked up the noisy street, dodging touts trying to drag us into bars and sidestepping piles of vomit as we went. There was a sign outside one place, which read:

All you can drink in an hour for 1,000 pesetas.

That was about four quid. No wonder things got so messy around here.

Away from the centre, things quietened down a bit. The bars were quieter, with many of them catering to the local population.

"This looks like the sort of place," said Nick.

It was an old-fashioned British style boozer called The Crown, with a picture of Queen Elizabeth II on the sign. There was a blackboard outside advertising that they showed *Only Fools and Horses* videos daily. A collection of red-faced, middle-aged, overweight men and their wives were sitting at the outside tables, drinking lager and gin and tonics.

"Perfect," I said.

Inside, the pub was decorated with Union Jack and St. George's Cross bunting, plus football scarves from various British clubs. There was also a wall covered with old banknotes, from the old, green pound notes, to some pre-decimal ones I had never seen before such as the ten-shilling note. This bar looked as if it had been here long before the clubbing scene came to town.

We could tell it was a bar for the resident Brits on the island by the way everyone looked at us when we went inside. It wasn't exactly hostile, but the implication was clear - what were we doing there? Club 18-30 holidaymakers simply never strayed into a place like this. The regulars in here were about as far removed from the clubbing crowd as you could imagine.

A couple was sitting at the bar who looked like part of the furniture. He was a stout, late middle-aged man with jet black hair, wearing a florid, yellow shirt. The top two buttons were undone, revealing a generous spread of chest hair and the obligatory medallion that some men of his vintage liked to wear. The bling spread to his fingers which were adorned with ostentatious, oversized rings.

His partner was doused in layers of make-up, including deep ruby red lipstick of the type favoured by women of dubious virtue. She was sipping from an impossibly large gin class, leaving red marks all over the rim. Her hair was immaculate styled into a blonde beehive, unlike his, which was an obvious hairpiece. You could even see the join. If I had to guess their ages, I would have put them at mid-sixties.

Despite his age, he looked like he could handle himself. You could imagine he was the sort of man who wouldn't take kindly to the question "Is that a wig?"

We walked over to the bar, right next to where they were sitting, and ordered a couple of beers. Then I attempted to engage them in conversation.

"Nice little pub, this," I ventured to the man.

"Bit off the track for you boys, isn't it?" he replied in a strong cockney accent. "I would have thought you'd have been more at home down the West End.

"Oh, we just fancied a change," I replied. "All that clubby music gets a bit repetitive after a while. May I buy you and your good lady a drink?"

"Well, that's very kind of you, uh…"

"I'm Thomas, and this is Nick," I replied.

"A delight to meet you, Tom, Nick," he replied. "I'm Trevor and this is Joan."

"Nice to meet you boys," she said, and winked at me, in a flirtatious manner.

Fortunately, Trevor didn't seem to notice. I wasn't too happy about him shortening my name to Tom as I had always preferred Thomas. I decided it might be best not to correct him.

"I'll have a large scotch if that's alright, and Joan will have a double gin and tonic."

"Careful," said Joan, giggling. "You know what I'm like when I've had a few drinks. I'm anybody's."

She looked like she had already had more than a few drinks. Once we had been served, we got chatting. It turned out that they were, as we had suspected, ex-pats. They sounded very well-heeled judging by their references to their villa, cars, and boats.

"So, what exactly was it you did for a living before you moved out here, Trevor?" I asked.

"Best not to ask, son," said Trevor, tapping his finger to his nose. "Let's just say I had my fingers in lots of pies and I had to move down here pretty sharpish if you catch my drift."

"Ah, you mean, you won't be popping back to London for a visit any time soon?" asked Nick.

"Got it in one, lad," he said. "I miss the old place, to tell the truth. You can't beat going to watch the Hammers on a Saturday afternoon. Now then, I'm still curious as to why you two lads are in here with us old-timers rather than chasing skirt in the clubs."

"Indeed," said Joan. "A pair of young studs like you shouldn't have any difficulty pulling the birds."

"You'd be surprised," said Nick. "We've been here all week and I've had no joy. He's done alright, though," he added, gesturing at me, with a hint of jealousy.

"Hmm, well maybe we ought to do something about that," said Joan.

That suggestion made me a little uncomfortable and I tried to change the subject.

"The reason we came in is that we're looking for someone," I said. "A friend of mine who flew out here to Ibiza from Cardiff this morning. We were meant to meet her in town tonight, but she's nowhere to be seen."

"And you thought she might be in here?" asked Trevor. "How old is this friend? Look around you, there's no-one other than you in here under fifty!"

"Not exactly," I said. "We think she may have been abducted by someone at the airport. We were hoping maybe someone like yourself who lives on the island might know something."

"Who would abduct her?" asked Trevor.

"Have you heard of the actor, Ben Lewis?" asked Nick.

"Oh, yeah, we know him alright! Big-headed, noisy arsehole!"

"You've seen him, then?" asked Nick. "You know where he is?"

It looked like we might have a lead.

"Oh, we know where he is, alright," said Trevor. "We can take you straight to him."

"Can we go now?" I asked impatiently, thinking it might not be too late to rescue her from his clutches.

"Woah, what's all the hurry?" asked Trevor. "The night's still young."

"I know, but it's really important we find her, as soon as possible," I replied. "We think she might be in danger."

He looked us both up and down, weighing up the situation.

"Tell you what, lads. I can see you're keen to find your friend, so how about this. I'll help you out if you help me out. A favour for a favour – just how we used to do it back in London in the good old days."

What could we possibly have that he would want, I thought? Then Joan winked at me again, and I had a worrying thought. No, he couldn't mean what I was thinking, could he?

"What did you have in mind?" asked Nick, eagerly. I don't think he had twigged yet.

"Well, you see, it's like this," he said. "I've had a bit of trouble with the old ticker this past year or two, and it means there are certain things I used to do, that I can't do anymore if you know what I mean?"

He cast his eyes in Joan's direction as he spoke. I glanced across too and saw her smiling at me. She leaned forward a little, giving a more revealing glimpse of her ample cleavage.

He did mean what I was thinking!

"Umm, I'm not entirely sure what you're driving at," I replied, lamely.

"Allow me to spell it out in black and white. Joan here, she's a woman with needs. She's always had a large appetite. Back home we were members of the Hackney swinger's association, but out here, regular partners are hard to find. Now what I'm proposing is that you two lads come back to our villa tonight and see to Joan's needs. Then I'll take you straight to Ben Lewis first thing in the morning. What do you say?"

I looked across at Nick who looked horrified. I doubt this is what he had in mind when he came to Ibiza on the pull. It certainly wasn't what I'd envisaged either. But desperate times called for desperate measures. I would do anything to find Sarah and these two were our only lead.

"We'll do it!" I declared, much to Nick's consternation.

"What both of us?" asked Nick.

"Oh, yes, both of you," said Joan, smiling. "I'm feeling exceptionally hungry tonight."

"Nice one, lads," said Trevor. "Now I think we'd better drink these up and go back to the villa. We wouldn't want you getting a case of the old brewers droop, would we?"

"You are sure you know where Ben Lewis is, aren't you?" I asked.

"My word is my bond, son," replied Trevor. "That's all that was ever needed back in the old East End."

The deal was done. Nick was looking at me in resigned disbelief, scarcely able to believe what I had got him into. We finished our drinks and Trevor drove us back to their luxury villa in his jeep. I won't go into the messy details suffice to say that we completed our business with his wife, as he watched.

Thankfully, we weren't expected to spend the entire night with her. Once it was over, we were shown to a spare room with two twin beds by a grateful Trevor. He was now treating us as if we were his two best friends. It was all very surreal.

As soon as Trevor left the room, Nick rounded on me.

"What the hell are you playing at, agreeing to that! I feel physically sick. She's nearly as old as my gran!"

"I can't see what the problem is, mate," I replied. "You've been moaning all week that you haven't had a shag since we arrived in Ibiza. Well, now you've had one."

"But with that! And I had to go after you. That means I've got…oh, I can't even bring myself to say it. I need a shower, and fast."

"Come on, it wasn't that bad," I said. "We all have to take one for the team occasionally."

"Yes – but for what? I said I'd go along with this Sarah thing, but this could just be some insane fantasy of yours."

"I promise, it is not a fantasy. You'll see."

"OK, that aside, what about this Trevor character? How much do we know about him? The way he's been talking tonight, he's coming across like some sort of gangster. What if he doesn't come through for us tomorrow? He might have other plans for us. You know what these people are like. Once you get sucked into their world it's hard to get out."

"Relax," I said. "Trevor's sound. Even if he is a gangster, these people have a sense of fair play. Salt of the Earth, most of them. I read a book about the Krays a while back. Proper gentleman, they were."

"I'm sure that thought will be of great comfort to me when I'm sinking to the bottom of the Mediterranean in lead boots!" he replied.

I had to admit, such misgivings had crossed my mind and I hoped my theory about Trevor's honourable credentials were right. I wasn't going to admit that to Nick, though.

"It'll be fine. Let's get some sleep," I said. "We can't do anymore tonight."

It took me a while to fall asleep, especially having to listen to Nick's snoring. He had gone out like a light. I wasn't happy about having to wait until morning. I'd have preferred to have found and confronted Ben tonight. Every hour he spent with Sarah was dangerous. What was he telling her? What might they be doing? I tried not to think about some of the possibilities, but I couldn't get the images out of my mind.

Eventually, fitfully, I slept, awaking some hours later to the morning sun pouring into the room. I leapt up immediately, roused Nick, and pulled on my jeans.

"Come on, we need to get up," I urged, as he groggily came to his senses.

We made our way out into the kitchen, where a contented looking Joan was laying out various breakfast items on the table. There was a welcome smell of something sweet baking and a coffee pot gurgling away.

"Morning, boys!" she said breezily. "Sleep well? I certainly did."

Nick cast me a worried look, which I picked up on immediately as did she.

"Relax, you're quite safe. You gave me more than enough last night. All I'm hungry for this morning is food, and I'm sure you are too. Coffee?"

"I'd love one," said Nick, with a look of palpable relief on his face.

"Help yourselves," she said, and we made our way over to the table where there was a selection of juices, yoghurt, fruit, and various pastries.

"Try the croissants," she said. "I baked them myself this morning."

It all looked extremely appetising, and we tucked in. As we ate, Trevor wandered in, now clad immaculately in a white cotton shirt and matching trousers. He was dressed perfectly for a summer day on the island.

We exchanged brief pleasantries before he brought up the subject of Ben.

"Now then, lads, I haven't forgotten my side of the bargain. You're looking for someone, and I know where he is."

"Where?" I asked impatiently.

"As luck would have it, next door. He moved in a few days ago. I haven't seen the owner for ages. He mainly uses it as a holiday home so I'm assuming Ben is a friend of his and he is letting him stay there."

"That's a stroke of luck. What are the chances of that, eh?" said Nick.

"It's not as much of a coincidence as you might imagine," said Trevor. "You saw last night when we arrived this is the most upmarket area on the island. Luxurious villas like this don't come cheap and there aren't that many of them. I'm rich. He's rich. It stands to reason we would end up in the same neighbourhood."

It made sense. I wondered what level of villainy Trevor had performed in his previous life to have afforded all this. He must be a multi-millionaire.

"Of course, when I say next door, his place is a couple of hundred yards away. Places this size come with plenty of land.

"We had better get going, then," said Nick.

"Woah, slow down," said Trevor. "Don't go at it like a bull in a china shop. These things need careful handling. I wouldn't be where I am today if I'd acted impulsively in my career. If this Ben has abducted your friend, we need to figure out how best to deal with him. Another half an hour isn't going to make a huge difference, so let's have another coffee and plan this properly."

I was more impatient to get started than Nick but reluctantly agreed. Over the next half hour, it became clear that

Trevor was an extremely useful ally. It was equally clear that he was not the sort of person you would want as an enemy. Especially after he told us a couple of grisly anecdotes about people who had crossed him. Unsurprisingly, they were no longer around to tell the tale.

Half an hour later Nick and I were outside the front of the neighbouring villa, with our plan all laid out. Nick was going to create a diversion at the front door while I sneaked around the back. Ben didn't know him, so hopefully, he would be able to occupy him long enough for me to search for Sarah.

Quite what I was going to say to her when I did, I had no idea. If she was a willing participant in all this, how was I going to persuade her she had got the wrong man? What did I have that could compete with a billionaire superstar?

All I could hope was that whatever it was that had drawn us together in that other timeline was powerful enough to win the day here. My faith in this wasn't particularly scientific, but then it never had been. This lifelong quest for Sarah had been akin to a religious ideology at times, and now the moment of revelation was upon me.

I made my way down the side of the villa, alongside perfectly manicured gardens, towards the rear of the building. I crept cautiously around the far corner, revealing a large patio and swimming pool area, and headed towards the large glass, rear doors.

As I did so, I heard the front doorbell ring. Two more steps and I would be at the glass door and would be able to see inside. As I took those last steps, I offered up a silent prayer to whoever might be listening.

Please, let her be there, and let her be safe.

The rest would be up to me.

Chapter Fifteen - Sarah

Sam and I were standing in the doorway between the hallway and the kitchen as Ben slowly opened the front door.

"Who are you and what do you want?" he barked rudely at whoever was outside. Ben had only opened the door to around forty-five degrees, to ensure he kept us out of sight of the caller.

"Hi, my name's Nick," said the unseen man. "I'm from the local resident's association and we noticed you'd just moved in. We were wondering if you might be interested in joining us."

"No, I would not," said Ben, abruptly.

"Oh, that's a shame," said Nick, breezily. "As we really do have lots of functions that might interest you. Or perhaps your good lady wife?"

"There's only me here," said Ben. "And anyway, I'm not a resident. I'm just staying here for a few weeks while the owner is away."

"Well, perhaps if I could just come in," said Nick, pushing forward.

As Ben blocked his path, Sam looked at me, and whispered, "maybe we should call out?"

"No, it's too risky," I said looking at the gun bulging in Ben's back pocket.

"Or we could run for it, out the back?"

"But the doors are locked," I replied.

"There must be a key somewhere," said Sam. "Or a window we can climb out of."

It was tempting. I looked back through the doorway to the kitchen patio doors and was surprised to see a man trying to open them, without success. He saw me looking at him and flashed me a beaming smile. Then he put his fingers to his lips to tell us to be quiet.

I looked back towards the front door where Ben was still arguing with Nick. He didn't seem to be having much luck trying to get rid of his unwanted visitor.

"What the bloody hell do you want a resident's association up here for anyway?" Ben was asking. "There are only a dozen or so villas and they're hundreds of yards apart. Plus, I can't imagine the sort of people who live here are particularly interested in coffee mornings with the neighbours."

"Stay here," I said, gesturing towards the rear door. Sam turned and caught sight of the mysterious stranger for the first time.

I turned and ran towards the patio doors, hoping that Ben was distracted enough not to turn around. I looked around frantically for the key, checking every surface, and looking in the kitchen drawers. The man was still at the window and gestured at me to hurry but it was to no avail. There was no key to be seen.

"No, you bloody can't, now piss off!" I heard Ben shout and the front door was slammed shut.

"Help," I mouthed silently through the door to the man, hoping he could lip read. "We're being kept prisoner."

"Where is she?" I heard Ben shout at Sam.

"Hide! He's coming back," I urged the stranger, who signalled his understanding by moving out of view.

"I thought I told you to stay where I could see you," said Ben, from the kitchen doorway. Once again, he had the gun in his right hand.

"Sorry," I said. "It's just so hot in here, I wanted to open a window for some fresh air."

"Don't give me that, you were trying to escape," he said. "Looking for this, were you?"

He reached into his pocket and produced the key. Thankfully, he wasn't showing any indication that he had spotted the mysterious stranger who had been at the window. I had no idea who he was, or what his intentions were, but he had looked friendly enough.

He was also just about the only hope we had right now. I needed to persuade Ben to open this door so decided to try a different approach.

"Look, there's no need for all this unpleasantness," I said, softening my tone. "Guns and stuff. It's all got a bit out of hand don't you think? I liked you before you started getting all possessive. Maybe we could stay a little longer. What do you think, Sam?"

She had seen the stranger too, so hopefully, she would realise what I was up to and play along.

"Yes, I guess we could stay another day, and maybe go back to the hotel tomorrow," suggested Sam. She cast me a brief glance to show she understood.

"What's behind this sudden change of heart?" asked Ben, suspiciously.

"Oh, come on, chill out," said Sam. "Sarah's right, we all got off on the wrong footing. It's a lovely day so let's go and hang out by the pool like we did yesterday."

"I don't trust you, Sam," said Ben. "You've been off with me from the start. I'm sorry, but this doesn't ring true."

"Look, if you don't trust us, bring your gun with you. We are not going to go crying for help like some helpless maidens in distress. This is the 1990s don't you know? We're made of stronger stuff than that."

"I'm not stupid enough to fall for that," said Ben. "Lull me into a false sense of security so I let my guard down – is that the plan?"

"Oh, come on, what else are we going to do?" I replied. "Sit around indoors all day? If we must stay here, we may as well enjoy ourselves. And, who knows, if you start being a bit nicer, I might be nice to you again tonight, if you know what I mean?"

The thought of having sex with this snake again now he had shown his true colours made my skin crawl. It was all a ruse because experience over the years had taught me that men would do almost anything if there was an offer of sex on the table.

It worked, because Ben acquiesced, allowing us to go and change into our swimsuits. He waited for us outside the bedroom door, which gave Sam and me no opportunity to talk to each other. No matter, I knew we were on the same wavelength. I may not have been able to talk, but I did now have a few moments to think.

Was the man at the door really who he had claimed to be, and who had been the man at the window? The two had to be connected. Perhaps it had been a classic distraction crime where Nick's job had been to keep Ben talking while the other man crept in the back and robbed the place. It was a feasible scenario apart from one thing.

The man I had spoken to didn't strike me as a burglar. He looked like a regular, young guy; a holidaymaker, just like us. And an attractive one, at that. I could have quite fancied him in less desperate circumstances.

Whoever he was, he offered the possibility of rescue. Despite Sam banging on all the time about girl power and looking after ourselves, I wasn't going to turn down assistance from this man if he was still around. We needed all the help we could get right now.

If he had understood what was happening, then once outside, he might be able to tackle Ben. However, there was the not inconsiderable problem of the gun, which he probably wouldn't know about.

Would Ben shoot him if he confronted him? I couldn't rule that possibility out. I know in the US you have the right to defend your property, but I had no idea how the law worked in Spain. It wasn't the sort of thing you read up on when you were planning a holiday.

As soon as we were changed into our bikinis, we headed back into the kitchen. Ben unlocked the door and slid the glass doors open. He gestured for us to go outside, still holding the gun.

I went first and saw the man from earlier standing next to the doors, with his back flat against the wall so he couldn't be seen from inside. I wanted to warn him about the gun, but I couldn't say anything without alerting Ben.

Sam was directly behind me, followed by Ben. As soon as he emerged, the man rushed forward to try and surprise him, but Ben was quick on the draw. Before he could tackle him, Ben pointed the gun right in his face, stopping him cold.

Then, an enormous grin spread across Ben's face.

"Thomas!" he exclaimed. "I can't tell you how delighted I am to see you. Once again, you have well and truly made my day."

"You know this man?" I asked.

"Oh, I know him, alright," replied Ben. "You would know him too by now if I hadn't intercepted you at the airport."

"What are you talking about?" I asked, at a loss as to what he meant. "What is going on here?"

"This, sweetheart, is the love of your life," he replied. "Or so he's been telling me for the past ten years."

I looked at the man he had called Thomas again. I couldn't deny I found him attractive, but there was no flicker of recognition.

"You must be mistaken. I've never seen him before in my life!"

"You may not have seen him, but he's certainly seen you," said Ben. "Thomas claims to have been reincarnated and that he's been dreaming for years about a previous life he spent with you. He has spent his entire life waiting for the special moment he was destined to meet you. According to him, this was right here in Ibiza and then you were going to get married and live happily ever after."

"Sounds like some sort of stalker to me," said Sam.

"Yes, that's it!" said Ben, seizing on Sam's lead and running with it. "He's a stalker and that's the reason I brought you both here and have been trying to stop you leaving. It was all for your protection. I think that makes me a bit of a hero, don't you?"

"Don't listen to him," warned Thomas. "This man is the most selfish, greedy and morally deficient man I have ever known."

"Yeah, that's not the sort of thing you want to be saying to a man pointing a gun at you, is it?" said Ben.

"You haven't got the guts to use that," said Thomas. "You're all talk, always have been."

"Oh, am I?" asked Ben. "If I'm all talk, how come my life is so much better than yours? I've got more money than you, shagged more women than you, and I'm more famous than you. And what have you got?"

"I've got my integrity, which is something you'll never have," replied Thomas.

I watched the battle of words between the men intently, keen to see where it would go. I had to say that Thomas was impressing me with his poise, particularly considering that he was the one at the wrong end of the gun.

"Who needs integrity?" asked Ben. "If I had an ounce of that, I wouldn't have had your woman last night!"

He had an immense look of self-satisfaction on his face as he delivered this news.

"What?" asked Thomas, looking distraught. He had been winning the argument until that point, but now his confidence was visibly draining away as Ben stuck the boot in.

"Oh, yes, your precious little Welsh tart over there. I did far more than just pick her up from the airport yesterday. I brought her back here, charmed the arse off her and then banged her. And do you know what? I savoured every single moment of it. It was the sweetest possible revenge for all the crap you've given me over the years!"

I was not happy about being called a Welsh tart, but my concern was more for Thomas at this moment. He looked aghast and I couldn't help feeling sorry for him. For a moment this all felt very real, but then I had to remind myself, I had never met Thomas before, even if I felt a curious connection to him.

These men were fighting over me, but it was a strange, fictional me that they had built some strange fantasy around. I had no idea what their motivations were or how I had become embroiled in their crazy world but involved I was. Where would it go next?

Thomas looked across at me and said, "Is this true, Sarah?"

I didn't get a chance to answer immediately because Ben interrupted again.

"Oh, it's true, alright! I've had your woman, just like you had mine. What goes around comes around. Hey, you never know, maybe I got her up the duff, just like you impregnated Charlotte. Karma's a bitch, mate!"

"What's he talking about?" I asked. This was getting more confusing by the minute.

"It's a long story," said Thomas, looking at me. Despite the perilous situation, he smiled and added: "Hopefully, I'll get a chance to tell you at some point."

"That all depends, doesn't it?" said Ben. "On what I decide to do with you."

As he was speaking, we saw another man appear from behind the far corner of the villa. Sam, Thomas, and I could all see him, but Ben couldn't. He had his back to him as he continued to keep the gun trained on the three of us.

I tried extremely hard not to give any indication I had noticed the man approaching Ben from behind. I took an educated guess that this was Nick, the man we had heard, but not seen, at the front door earlier.

Sam waded back into the conversation, keeping Ben distracted, and speaking loudly for the benefit of Nick.

"Come on, Ben, this is ridiculous," said Sam. "You're not going to shoot us, now let's just stop all this nonsense and go our separate ways. I've no idea what sort of feud is going on between you two or why you chose to drag us into it, but this charade has gone on long enough."

That was clever. It was her way of alerting Nick that Ben had a gun. He was still creeping up behind him, but slowed his pace, becoming increasingly cautious so as not to be heard.

"I could shoot you all if I wanted to," shouted Ben. "I'm one of the richest men in the world. I can do whatever the hell I want!"

"Excuse me," said Nick, right in his ear. "But you really should have agreed to join the resident's association."

He caught Ben completely by surprise. He whirled around, momentarily confused, and Nick punched him squarely in the face.

He fell backwards, but just about maintained his balance, still clutching the gun. Provided he had that in his hand, we were all in danger. But before he could turn it back upon us, Sam found a huge surge of courage.

She leapt forward and with a karate-style move, kicked it out of his hand, sending it scuttling across the patio, towards the far side of the pool. I had never seen her move so fast. It was amazing what a little adrenalin could do in a tricky situation.

"You twats, I swear I'll kill the lot of you," he shouted, regaining his balance, and casting his eyes around to try and locate the gun. All of us had had the same idea and joined in a mad sprint across the patio to where the gun had come to rest. It was at the base of the low stone wall that marked the boundary to the property.

Ben was marginally ahead. We couldn't let him get there before us. I honestly don't believe he would have killed us before, but he was riled now. In the heat of the moment, anything could happen. For the first time since this had started, I sensed we were in mortal danger.

He reached the wall just before the rest of us and reached down for the gun, but he was too slow. The rest of us arrived as one and piled into him like rugby players into a ruck. The wall was little more than a metre high, and the combined force of the four of us was enough to send him straight over.

I had been at the front of the group and was catapulted on to the wall. I tried desperately to find something to grab hold of before I too went over the edge. I knew that the sea lay beyond the wall, but I hadn't looked directly over before and had no idea that there was a sheer drop on the other side.

Despite the situation, the first thought in my head was how dangerous it was, and that the builders should have built the wall higher. What if there had been kids here? I was swiftly distracted from that by the scream that was now assaulting my eardrums. It was from Ben who was now hurtling down the cliff.

Then the scream cut off as he crashed onto a path that jutted out from the cliff edge, some thirty feet below. There was an audible, bone-shattering thud. At the same time, I felt a pair of strong arms pulling me back from the wall.

"It's all right, I've got you now," said Thomas.

Chapter Sixteen - Thomas

Ben had fallen over the cliff and I'd saved Sarah from suffering the same fate. I felt quite the dashing hero, vanquishing the enemy, and winning the girl's heart at the end of the film. It was all rather exhilarating, but I didn't want to get carried away. I hadn't quite got the girl yet.

As I pulled Sarah back from the edge, I caught her gaze, and that's when I felt the spark between us. Her eyes were awash with relief and gratitude, but I knew it wasn't only that. There was definitely a connection.

It was a different place and a different time from where we should have met, but her look was just as I had always pictured it. I was confident now that things were going to work out, but for the moment, we had a more pressing issue to deal with.

Ben had fallen at least forty feet on to a stony path further down the cliff. He wasn't moving and even this far away, I could see a pool of blood seeping from his head. He was clearly done for.

I am a compassionate person, for the most part, but I felt not a hint of remorse in this instance. Ben had been a vile individual, with no redeeming features. He had abused the powers that time had bestowed upon him without a care for the people he trampled underfoot in pursuit of his selfish ends.

Unfortunately, none of that was going to count for much in a court of law. We still had a dead body to deal with. Conveniently, we had a friend who was an expert in these matters close at hand.

"It looks like you've got a bit of a problem there, lads," came the welcome voice of Trevor behind us.

After showing us Ben's villa, we had assumed he had gone back to his place, but instead, he had stuck around. Unseen by us, he had wandered around the corner of the building during the scuffle and was now looking at the four of us peering guiltily over the wall.

"Did you…?" I began to ask.

"Oh, I saw," said Trevor. "But don't worry. He got what he deserved if you ask me. The question is, what are you going to do now?"

I looked over the wall again. Although I could see across the bay to the beach a couple of miles away, it was still early in the day and almost deserted. The Ibiza club crowd kept late hours, and few had surfaced yet.

"I don't think anyone else saw," I said.

"They will soon if you don't move him," said Trevor.

"Perhaps we ought to call the authorities," suggested Sam.

"And tell them what?" said Trevor. "It was an accident? Do you want to take that chance? I wouldn't. You need to deal with this yourselves."

"Is it even possible to get down there?" asked Sam.

"For sure, that path winds up and down to the sea," replied Trevor. "You can access it from the back gate to my place."

"So, what do we do then?" I asked. "Go down, get his body, and then what?"

"We get rid of it," said Trevor. "Remember, I was brought up amongst the East End's finest. Let's just say I have a little experience of this sort of thing. You lads did me a favour last night, so the least I can do is help you out. That's how we used to do things back in the old days."

"Thank-you, we would appreciate the help," I said hurriedly. I hoped he didn't go into any details about the favour we had done for him in front of Sarah. To be fair, while that had been going on, she had been having sex with Ben, but I could hardly blame her for that. She hadn't known what she was getting into.

The sordid antics Nick and I had been forced to stoop to, were probably best not mentioned for now. Even if it had all been in a good cause.

"What are we going to do with the body, even if we can get it back up here?" asked Nick.

"Relax," said Trevor. "I've got a yacht moored down in the bay. We'll take him for a little cruise out to sea."

The next couple of hours were quite surreal. A small group of people, mostly strangers less than a day ago, were united by the necessity to dispose of a dead body, undetected.

It was hard work in the heat. It was only a short walk up the path to the back gate which led into Trevor's villa, but time was of the essence. Every second we delayed increased the danger that another resident of the area might come along.

The path was stony, narrow, and uneven, with a sheer drop on one side. Attempting to carry a body in such circumstances was fraught with danger. We were also in plain sight if anyone with a decent pair of binoculars on the other side of the bay happened to look this way.

It was too narrow for four of us to carry the body, so Nick and I had to do it between us. I had drawn the short straw, reversing back up the path, directed by the girls, and it was exhausting. It may only have been a couple of hundred yards, but it felt like miles and it took us a good half an hour.

Back at Trevor's villa, we packed the body into a large, square packing crate and loaded it onto the back of his pickup truck. All of this was done under the watchful eye of Joan who had come out to see what was going on. She didn't seem remotely fazed by having a dead body brought onto her property. Presumably, being married to Trevor, she was used to this sort of thing.

Nick and I, along with the two girls, took a corner each of the crate and lifted it on to the back of the pickup. Trevor said he couldn't help because of his heart condition.

"Why are we doing this in broad daylight?" asked Sam. "Wouldn't it be better to wait until after dark?"

"Time is of the essence in these situations," explained Trevor. "Once people realise that he's missing, they'll come looking for him. And he's not just any random guy. He's a celebrity and the paparazzi know he's on the island. If they figure out where he has been staying, you won't be able to move around here for photographers. We have to get rid of him now."

"Isn't it going to look a bit suspicious, us loading this great big crate on to a yacht?" asked Nick.

"With luck no-one will see us. My yacht's moored in a private bay just down below here. There are only three or four yachts moored there, and it's quiet most of the time."

"I hope we're not pushing our luck," said Sam. "I'm amazed we got him up here without being seen."

"We'll be fine," Trevor assured us. "Now, can you see that pile of bricks over there? They're left over from when I built our barbecue. Grab a few dozen of them and stick them on the truck. We'll need something to weigh the crate down with later."

Once that was done, we were on our way. Nick, Sarah, and I sat on the back of the truck, holding on to the crate, and trying not to think about what was inside. Meanwhile, Sam and Joan rode in the front with Trevor.

Joan had brought a large picnic basket along with her and was cheerily treating this as if we were on a day out. In contrast, those of us in the back of the truck were still quite numbed by the sequence of events. While Joan was banging on about Rioja and Serrano ham sandwiches, we were keeping tight hold of a box containing a dead body.

I looked across to try and catch Sarah's eye but the task at hand was hardly conducive to romance. Despite the breeze wafting over us as Trevor drove down towards the bay, it was still baking hot, and I could feel beads of sweat forming on my forehead.

I wondered how long it would be in this heat until the body started to smell. There were already clouds of small flies circling around us. They were trying to keep up with the truck as it bounced around on the stony, dusty track that led down towards the shore.

I tried to strike up a conversation with Sarah to lighten the mood, but it was stilted, and I struggled. I needed to connect with her as soon as possible. Right now, we were all in this together and she wasn't going anywhere, but what would happen when all this was over? Despite my earlier confidence, there was still a nagging worry that she might not want any more to do with me.

It only took about five minutes for us to arrive at the bay. There was only one road in, which was barely more than a cracked, earthen track by the end. Cliffs rose on either side, and the pine trees that grew all around provided a natural and welcoming shelter.

Trevor's impressive-looking yacht was anchored alongside a small jetty. It was painted claret and blue, I am guessing in honour of West Ham, and sported the name *The Jellied Eel*. He certainly missed his old life in the East End. It was the only craft there so presumably whoever else used the bay wasn't around. It was very secluded, and I was able to relax a little. We had made it this far and it was unlikely anyone would see us now.

The task of getting the crate on to the yacht wasn't easy. Ben's dead body seemed to be getting heavier the hotter the day got. We just about managed it, despite a couple of mishaps which were reminiscent of an old Laurel and Hardy film involving a piano. Once it was finally aboard, we all felt a palpable sense of relief.

"Now we head out to sea," announced Trevor. "About twenty miles should be far enough."

"In the meantime, how about a drink?" asked Joan. "I imagine you all need one after that. Come below decks, we've got a fully-stocked bar."

"That's the best suggestion I've heard all day," said Nick. I felt a bit sorry for him. I had dragged him through an awful lot this past day or so and vowed that I would make it up to him.

"I've got some ice-cold San Miguel down here," she replied, which sounded good to me. After what we'd been through, I could sink a barrel full.

I just hoped Joan wasn't going to get drunk and demand a repeat performance of the previous evening. They had just done us another enormous favour and knowing how Trevor's barter system worked, we might be in their debt again.

Beers in hand, we returned to the upper deck and made our way round to the bow, as far away as possible from the crate at the stern. Finally, this gave me a chance to talk to Sarah alone.

It was bright in the midday sun, enhanced by the reflection which was shimmering off the surface of the sea which meant I almost had to squint to see her. I thought about my sunglasses which were sitting uselessly back in our hotel room where I'd left them when we had gone out the previous evening. An awful lot had happened since then.

"Well, this wasn't quite how I'd envisaged our first day together," I said. It turned out not to be the best of opening lines.

"Yeah, that still sounds a little stalkerish to me," she replied. "All that stuff Ben said about you planning your whole life around meeting me here in Ibiza. Do you know how creepy that sounds?"

"I realise that," I admitted. "But look at everything's that's happened. Ben went to an awful lot of effort to keep you away from me, and why would he do that? You know the sort of man he was. He certainly wasn't doing it for any noble intentions."

"It was a horrible experience," she admitted. "I feel bloody stupid being so easily duped by him."

"Don't be too hard on yourself. He was a huge star, and it's easy to be blinded by that. But it's over now. As for you and me, well I'm not a stalker, and if you want to walk away from all this, I'm not going to pursue you. Unlike Ben, I don't believe in manipulating people."

"Walking away might be a little tricky," she said, smiling. "We're in the middle of the sea, miles from anywhere. Where could I go?"

I smiled back, looking directly into her eyes, and again felt the connection between us. I knew she was feeling it too."

"I haven't had a proper chance to explain all this yet," I replied. "But since, as you've just said, we're not going anywhere for a while, why don't you let me tell you my side of the story? Then when we get back on dry land it's entirely up to you whether you want to stick around or not."

"I am curious as hell about all of this," she said. "Come on then, tell all. Then I'll tell you what I think. Don't hold anything back."

I looked across the deck to where Nick and Sam were eagerly devouring a jug of punch that Joan had rustled up. They seemed to be getting on well. I had promised him that they would. Perhaps if he had a little fun with her, he might forgive me for dragging him into this situation.

I started by telling Sarah the story of Terry French falling off the climbing frame all those years ago.

I told her of the dreams I'd had of her and me in the future. I also explained my resolve not to disrupt the timeline and how Ben's appearance on the scene had interfered with all of that.

I was a little uneasy when I came on to the subject of the events that led to my impregnation of Charlotte, and that I was already a father. I decided to tell her anyway. What was the point of holding back something that she would have to know about sooner or later? She seemed sympathetic to that and continued to engage enthusiastically with me.

Gaining in confidence, I explained all that had happened since we had arrived in Ibiza and the lengths we had gone to find her. I even included the sordid encounter with Joan the previous night, without which we would never have found her.

She wasn't offended by this revelation at all. I was pleasantly surprised to find that she found it downright hilarious.

"You must love me if you were prepared to go to those lengths!" she exclaimed. "It seems that it's not just me that had an encounter last night they want to forget ever happened."

There was only one thing I decided to keep from her because it related to a future event in the timeline. I didn't tell her anything about Stacey. She was just about getting her head around the possibility that we were fated to be together.

If I added the news that within the next month, I would get her pregnant and that she would give birth to a daughter next year then she would probably run a mile. I could not possibly bring that up, not with the conversation going so well.

Our talk was brought to an abrupt end at that point because Trevor had decided we were far enough out to dispose of Ben's body. As the sound of the engines died, I looked back to see that Ibiza was now a distant rock on the horizon. We had reached Ben's final resting place.

Under Trevor's guidance, Nick and I loaded up the crate with bricks to ensure it would sink. Then, with Sarah and Sam's help, we prepared to launch my former nemesis over the side.

"Shouldn't we say a few words?" asked Sarah.

"Why would we?" replied Sam. "The man was an absolute monster. I doubt whether anyone will mourn his loss. It will probably be a relief to his wife that he's gone, for a start."

"She won't know that he's dead, though, will she?" said Nick. "Only the six of us here know that. As far as the rest of the world is concerned, he will have just disappeared."

"Quite right," said Trevor. It will be one of those great unsolved mysteries. He might become the Lord Lucan of his age. I'm sure it goes without saying, that no-one outside of the six of us here must ever know about this."

"Agreed," I replied, though secretly, I was thinking that I might tell Charlotte at some point. She had been an integral part of this after all and I knew I could trust her.

"Let's get it over with," said Nick.

With one final heave, the four of us pushed Ben over the side to his watery grave.

For a moment, it looked like the crate wasn't going to sink, as it bobbed about on the surface. Then, as it filled with water, it slowly began to submerge.

"Good riddance," said Sam, summing up what we all felt.

As Ben disappeared beneath the waves, I felt a sense of closure. I was finally free of him, and Sarah was by my side.

It was up to me now.

Chapter Seventeen - Sarah

Nearly twenty years had passed since that crazy week in Ibiza, which had changed my life forever. On the day I met him, my future husband had saved my life by preventing me from falling over a cliff. Now he had just done it again.

I had become used to his odd premonitions over the years, and this was the second time in the space of two years we had found ourselves in danger. Already, Thomas had saved our daughter, Stacey, from a horrifying ordeal at the hands of a potential rapist.

He had been having nightmares about what would happen to her for weeks beforehand if he did not intervene. Not only did he prevent the attack, but he was also able to frame the attacker and ensure he ended up behind bars where he couldn't harm anyone else.

Stacey was the most precious thing in our lives. She was conceived soon after we became lovers in the wake of the traumatic circumstances of our first meeting.

When we had first met, he had told me the tale of his previous life, in which we'd married and fallen in love. I initially dismissed this as some schoolboy fantasy, which he really should have grown out of at his age. If it had come from any other man, I would have dropped him like a ton of bricks.

But there was something curiously alluring about Thomas. I had never believed in all that soppy love at first sight nonsense. It certainly hadn't been that way with Gareth, or anyone else, but Thomas was different. There was an instant attraction, on both a physical and mental level, and it wasn't just because we'd been thrown together in the face of adversity.

I often think about what happened on that first day. It had begun in horrifying circumstances, that had culminated in me helping to dispose of a dead body in the Mediterranean. It was on that boat trip that Thomas and I got talking properly for the first time, and it was then that I knew I wanted to see him again.

After we had returned from our trip out to sea, Sam and I had finally made it to San Antonio and into our accommodation. We told the rep we had been so drunk on duty-free that we had somehow got lost on the way out of the airport. Then we had been on an all-night bender at a club. It wasn't as outrageous as it sounded as anyone who has ever been on a holiday of that type will testify.

We were staying in the same hotel as Thomas and Nick and naturally paired up with them for the rest of the week. There was a certain inevitability about what was going to happen and by the second day of the holiday, Thomas and I kissed for the first time, at a water party in the sunken dancefloor at *Es Paradis*. We were inseparable for the rest of the week and have been ever since.

It was hard to completely relax during those first few days. We had killed a man after all, despite the circumstances, and I was terrified that at some point the police would come calling. But nothing happened and the news of Ben's disappearance didn't even break until we were back in the UK.

When we returned home, I couldn't bear to be apart from Thomas. There was little left for me in Swansea, other than Sam, and I cast my life there aside to move to Oxford. There was no prospect of her following because she and Nick had nothing in common. They spent the week shagging each other in Ibiza, and then went back to their own lives. The next time they saw each other was at our wedding.

By now, I had completely accepted the strange nature of Thomas's existence. Any scepticism I may have had about his abilities was dispelled when he began making eerily accurate predictions about things that would happen on a day-to-day basis. He was always spot on and I was soon convinced.

He told me more about his life before he had met me. After I moved to Oxford, he introduced me to his ex, Charlotte, and their son, Jack. I found him to be a delightfully fun and cheeky nine-year-old and it didn't bother me that he had a child from a previous relationship.

I found Charlotte welcoming and easy to talk to and was fascinated to hear her side of the story. I particularly enjoyed the tales she had about Ben, especially the one about keying his car. Our mutual dislike of him helped us bond and we soon become firm friends.

My relationship with Thomas was tested a couple of months after we got together when I discovered I was pregnant.

It was a shock to me, but he didn't seem surprised in the slightest.

When I pressed him on the matter, he confessed that he had foreseen my pregnancy. It transpired that there was a whole part of our future that he had conveniently neglected to mention to me. We had a daughter in the future that he had known about the whole time.

"Why didn't you tell me?" I insisted. "You told me everything else. I trusted you."

"I didn't feel that I could," he replied. "I needed to let nature and the timeline take the correct course. If you had known you were going to fall pregnant, you might have tried to prevent it."

"And you didn't think that such a huge life-changing event was something you ought to have discussed with me? It's my body and my life – you don't get to make these decisions for me."

"Realistically, what would you have said?" he replied. "Think back to that day on the boat. We had barely met. Imagine if I had started talking about us being destined to have a baby together and that I wanted to get you pregnant. What would any woman have said in that situation?"

"OK, I concede you have a point but even so, I still feel a little manipulated by all of this. Is this what it's always going to be like? You always one step ahead of me, for the rest of our lives?"

"I promise you that this is a one-off," he tried to assure me. "In the future, I'll be open with you about everything."

"No wonder you were so damned keen. You couldn't get enough of me that week in Ibiza. We were at it like rabbits!"

"Just like any couple in a new relationship," he replied. "Look, I was just trying to keep everything the same as before. You didn't know you were going to get pregnant in this life, any more than you did in any of the others."

"No, and that's still a mystery. I know we were lax on the condoms, and that was unforgivable given all the STD's around these days, but I was on the pill too."

"Yes, and I also recall you overdoing it on the cocktails on at least two nights and ending up throwing up the next morning."

"That was probably it, then" I conceded. I had heard that being sick diminished the effectiveness of the contraceptive pill.

"My only worry now is that the baby might not be the same as I remember. I have clear memories of Stacey, not only what she looked like, but also her personality. I have no idea how that could be altered if you didn't get pregnant at the same place and time as before?"

"That's the least of our worries," I replied. "I shudder at having to bring this up, but as you know, to my eternal shame, I slept with Ben the night before I met you. What if it's his baby I'm carrying? He even bragged about that possibility before he died."

"Believe me, I've thought about it," he said. "I've lost sleep over it."

"You're not the only one," I replied. "Imagine how it feels knowing I might be carrying the bastard spawn of Satan in my belly. What if it's a boy and he turns out like him? How would we cope with that? Maybe I should consider a termination. We can always try for another baby, later."

"Don't say that in front of Charlotte," he replied. "She's fiercely opposed to abortion. Also, look at it from my perspective. I have memories of a baby, growing up to be a young woman, who you adored and were proud of. If we don't see this through, none of that will ever happen. You'll be denying Stacey her chance of life."

"And when she's born, what if she's different? Or a boy? Do we have DNA tests to see who's the father?"

"How are we supposed to get Ben's DNA?" asked Thomas. "Get a diving bell and go down to the seabed to pluck a hair from his corpse?"

"No, that's ridiculous," I replied. "All we need to do is have a test to see if you are the father or not. Don't worry, there aren't any other candidates. I'm not a total slag, you know."

"I never thought you were," he replied. "Ben manipulated you into bed that night. He had an unfair advantage."

"The same advantage that you have," I pointed out.

"There's one key difference," he said. "I use my powers for good, he used his for evil."

"When you put it like that you make it sound like a superhero film," I replied.

"Well, just be glad you ended up with the good guy."

"Oh, I am, believe me," I replied. "OK, cards on the table. I wasn't serious about having an abortion, I couldn't do that. But I do have some concerns. If when the baby is born, it's not what you're expecting, what then? Can you honestly say that you are willing to bring Ben's baby up as your own?"

"Sarah, I love you and as long as we're together we can overcome anything. And above all else, the baby is innocent in all this."

He sounded sincere, and I had no reason to doubt him. We left it there, and it was not mentioned again during the pregnancy though I knew it was still preying on both our minds. It was all very well going into this with good intentions, but how would he react if things didn't turn out as he hoped?

At the time of giving birth, I was too consumed with the pain to give much thought to whose baby it was, but when she was delivered and handed to me, I could tell from the sheer look of delight on Thomas's face that all was well.

"She's perfect!" he said. "Exactly as I pictured her. Welcome to the world, Stacey."

It was a huge relief for both of us, and from that point onwards, we were able to settle into a cosy, family life.

Thomas was a lot more relaxed now that the future was secure. He still had his premonitions, but for many years they were of a trivial, and often amusing nature - like the time Nick tripped and fell in the Thames after a few too many drinks at The Head of the River. Thomas could have stopped him but decided to let it happen anyway for comedy value.

When it came to events in the wider world, he rarely took advantage of his insights. All he had ever cared about was being together with me and Stacey and had no desire to pursue wealth in the way that Ben had. Occasionally he would relax these rules if it meant getting a little extra holiday money, but that was as far as it went.

We moved into a larger place, Thomas got promoted at work, and I decided to embark on a legal career, juggling parenting with studying for a law degree. We had a comfortable lifestyle, and only twice did we face danger again.

Both times, Thomas came to our rescue, saving first Stacey and then me. He had been having nightmares in the weeks running up to both incidents, waking in a sweat in the night, screaming at times. I managed to calm him, and we worked out how to deal with each situation and bring those responsible to justice.

We never had another child. Thomas had already told me he had no memories of another in his previous life. It didn't mean we couldn't try for one, but for whatever reason, it never happened.

Stacey never felt like an only child. Unlike in Thomas's previous life, she had her big brother Jack, who spent frequent weekends with us. He doted on and was very protective over her.

She grew up and got married, as did Jack, and soon both couples blessed our family with grandchildren.

Thomas's ability to see into the future disappeared as he got older. This left him unable to forecast the 2029 asteroid strike that unleashed a devastating freeze in the Northern Hemisphere.

A couple of years previously we had invested in a holiday home in the Canary Islands and were able to get the whole family out there before the worst of the weather struck. The villa was nowhere near as grandiose as the one which Ben had taken me to in Ibiza and it was a tight squeeze for the several months we had to stay there.

When we returned to Britain to see the havoc and death caused by the Black Winter, we knew we'd had a lucky escape.

Speaking of Ben, the mystery of his disappearance was never solved. All sorts of theories were put forward over the years, many wildly far from the truth. A lot of sordid stories came out after his death and few mourned him. Perhaps that was why there was little more than a half-hearted attempt from the authorities to find him.

From time to time, there were rumours that he had been spotted. One tabloid claimed on the front page, years later, that he was alive and well and living in a monastery in Tibet. None of these stories ever came to anything. We kept quiet as agreed in Ibiza that day, with one exception. Thomas felt that it was only right that we should tell Charlotte, and I agreed.

When I looked back on my life, I had no cause for complaint. Being with Thomas had hardly been conventional, but I had never regretted choosing to be with him. I knew very quickly in Ibiza that he was the right one, despite all the weird stuff he had come out with.

When you know, you just know, don't you?

Chapter Eighteen - Thomas

There is a final footnote to my tale, which happened one October day while we were walking along the coastline in Cornwall.

Sarah and I had long since retired and moved down to live in St Ives, possibly the prettiest seaside town in Britain.

Despite being in our early eighties now, we kept fit by walking regularly, enjoying all the weather that Cornwall had to offer. The year I turned eighty we spent several months walking the South West Coast Path, all 630 miles of it.

It was a typical, blustery autumn day as we walked along the coastline close to Zennor, a village a few miles from St Ives. The main tourist season was now over, and we saw few people other than a couple of local dog walkers.

Then we encountered a middle-aged man walking towards us. He didn't notice us immediately as he was intently studying the readout on a futuristic-looking device. It resembled a long, silver wand and he was pointing it towards the shore as if scanning for something.

As we approached, I felt a strong sense of déjà vu. It wasn't a premonition such as those that had defined my younger life. They had stopped abruptly in the mid-2020s.

This was different. The memory that had been triggered was of one of my previous visions from decades ago, 1990 to be precise. I had pictured meeting this man before, and I knew who he was. Perhaps I was finally going to get the answers I had been looking for all my life.

"Excuse me," I began. "Is your name Josh?"

The man looked back at me, slightly taken aback at being recognised.

"Maybe," he said, warily. "Who's asking?"

"My name's Thomas Scott," I replied. "Ring any bells?"

"Thomas!" he exclaimed. "It's so good to see you again! And alive and well, after all these years!"

"What do you mean by again?" I asked. "We've never met before. We were supposed to, but you never turned up."

"August 1990?" he asked.

"Yes," I replied. "I had a vision that you would be there. I flew all the way back from Greece to meet you. I was so disappointed when you didn't come."

"He can see the future," explained Sarah. "At least he used to be able to."

"I was there in 1990," insisted Josh. "But it's possible it may not have been in this universe. Once I started tinkering around with the multiverse, things started getting out of control. I've been to so many different universes, I've lost track. This isn't even the one I was born in."

"Sounds complicated," remarked Sarah.

"It is," replied Josh. "But I'm quite happy to try and explain it to you if you've time."

"Oh, I've time," I said. "You're only six decades late. I'm not letting you go until you do!"

"Do you fancy a cream tea?" asked Sarah. "There's a lovely little café back in Zennor. We often call in there after walking around here."

"I'd love one," replied Josh.

"That's settled then," said Sarah.

Over delicious scones, smeared with local clotted cream and jam, I finally got the answers I had been seeking my entire life.

I learned that the strange, backwards life I had previously lived had been as a direct result of a time travel accident that Josh had created. That had been my second life. In my first life, I had died in hospital in my fifties, at the end of a miserable life in which Sarah had also died at the hands of the drunk driver.

This confirmed what I had always suspected. This was my third life. It also explained why I couldn't remember anything from 2025 onwards. Dead men don't make memories.

Josh had enjoyed a lifetime of time travel adventures that had started with the discovery of a time bubble when he was still at school. When I asked him about Ben, he confirmed that he was responsible for sending him back to 1988.

"Yes, I am sorry about that," he said. "I was experimenting at the time with transferring consciousness back into people's past bodies. Unfortunately, just after I sent Ben back, I got embroiled in a catastrophe that almost destroyed the entire multiverse. By the time all that was sorted out, I was unable to retrieve him without risking further damage. I had no choice but to leave him where he was."

"He gave us no end of trouble," said Sarah.

"Again, my apologies," said Josh. "And for getting you two caught up in all this in the first place."

"Don't be," I replied. "If it hadn't been for you, Sarah and I would be long dead. Instead, not only are we both alive and well, but I've also had the luxury of living life three times over. How many people get that sort of opportunity? We have plenty to thank-you for."

"Don't mention it," he replied. "Now I must go because it's going to be dark in a couple of hours. There a time bubble in this area, and I've been picking up some strange readings from it. I need to go and check it out."

"I thought you were retired from time travelling now," I said.

"I am," he said. "But I need to remain vigilant. Someone somewhere is bound to discover how to time travel again at some point, and who knows what they might get up to.

I see it as my responsibility to keep an eye on these things because the consequences of people blundering about in time can be huge as you've both seen."

He bid us farewell, and left the café, leaving us to finish our tea.

I had enjoyed meeting Josh. He had left me with a sense of closure. I finally knew who I was and why everything had happened the way it had.

I looked across the table at Sarah, still as beautiful to me as she had ever been. We had been given the precious gift of decades of extra time we would never have had if it had not been for Josh's serendipitous intervention.

I smiled, reached for the pot, and poured us both another cup of tea.

THE END…for now, but the adventures will continue.

Reviews

Before you go, may I ask a small favour?

As an independent author, I don't have the strength of a big marketing budget behind me. I rely on word of mouth to spread the word about my books, plus genuine reviews from enthusiastic readers who have enjoyed the book. These help potential new readers decide whether or not to try a story from an author they haven't read before.

If you enjoyed these books, I would be hugely grateful if you would consider taking a few minutes to leave a short review on the Amazon website. Every little helps, even if it is only a couple of short sentences.

The Time Bubble Collection

If you missed any of the earlier books in the series, please head over to my author page on Amazon where you can find them individually, or in box sets:

1) The Time Bubble
2) Global Cooling
3) Man Out of Time
4) Splinters in Time
5) Class of '92
6) Vanishing Point
7) Midlife Crisis
8) Rock Bottom
9) My Tomorrow, Your Yesterday
10) Happy New Year
11) Return to Tomorrow

UK Link:

https://www.amazon.co.uk/Jason-Ayres/e/B00CQO4XJC/

US Link:

https://www.amazon.com/Jason-Ayres/e/B00CQO4XJC/

About the author

Jason Ayres lives in the market town of Evesham with his wife and two sons.

Following a lengthy career in market research, he turned his hand to writing whilst bringing up his children. This included the popular *Stay at Home Dad* column in the *Oxford Mail*.

Encouraged by this success, he moved on to writing time travel novels, releasing *The Time Bubble* in the summer of 2014. This original and well-received story has since developed into an epic series which shows no signs of stopping.

Want to know more about Jason?

You can find his official website here:

https://www.jasonayres.co.uk/

Find him on Twitter:

https://twitter.com/TheTimeBubble/

Or check out his Facebook page for the latest news:

https://www.facebook.com/TheTimeBubble/

Printed in Great Britain
by Amazon